EARTH-BOUND

Earth-Bound

& Other
Supernatural Tales

by

Dorothy Macardle

The Swan River Press
Dublin, Ireland
MMXX

Earth-Bound
by Dorothy Macardle

Published by
The Swan River Press
Dublin, Ireland
in September, MMXX

www.swanriverpress.ie
brian@swanriverpress.ie

Cover design by Meggan Kehrli from
"Farmyard Disused" (2015) © Brian Gallagher

Set in Garamond by Ken Mackenzie

Paperback Edition
ISBN 978-1-78380-738-3

Swan River Press published a limited edition
hardback of *Earth-Bound* in May 2016.

Contents

~

Mountjoy

How could I bear the night,
    Lying awake, alone,
Had I not thought of the Light
    Until my thought is grown
A stronger thing than the sun
    To summon beauty to birth
And ripen, when Winter's done,
    The Golden Age of the earth?

How could I bear the waste
    Of wind swept days of the Spring,
But that I've heard the haste
    Of a braver wind on the wing,
Out of the cave of the hours
    Flowing, potent and near
The wind that will wake the flowers,
    And with the hosts of fear?

How could we bear the death
    Of noble men in the dawn,
The volley that broke our breath,
    Their lives with the echoes gone;
But that we knew their blood
    Would cry from the altar-stone
Till the hearts of the multitude
    Grew as brave as their own?

They lie in a prison grave
    Dead, but they are not dumb;
Great is the price they gave;
    The end that they dreamed shall come,
And the call of their fearless voices
    And the sound of their proud farewell
Shall echo when Earth rejoices
    That Heaven has conquered Hell.

Introduction

It could be argued that the stories in this volume would never have been written had Dorothy Macardle not languished as a political prisoner in Dublin's Mountjoy Gaol, and then Kilmainham Gaol. Following on that logic, it might also be suggested that without making these short forays into supernatural fiction she might never have produced her classic ghost/detective novel *Uneasy Freehold* (Peter Davis, 1941), which became more popular under its re-title, *The Uninvited*, to tie-in with the 1944 film adaptation starring Ray Milland and Ruth Hussey, afterwards adapted for radio, stage, and translated into several languages.

It has been on that novel her literary reputation, rightly or wrongly, rests. But it is an injustice that her other fiction has all but been forgotten. Her respectable body of work, her plays, novels, short stories, serials, and poems, are now neglected. Even those plays that were premiered at the Abbey and Gate theatres have not been performed since her death; yet her work was well received in her lifetime.

A factor that has helped to eclipse her literary work in Ireland has been her seminal history *The Irish Republic: A Documented Chronicle of the Anglo-Irish Conflict and the Partitioning of Ireland with a Detailed Account of the Period 1916-1923* (Gollancz, 1937), to which Éamon de Valera wrote an introduction.

Unfortunately, Dorothy has also been badly served in the field of biography where often popular legend and personal prejudice have replaced fact and a fair assessment of one of Ireland's most fascinating writers.

Before one can appreciate the background to the current stories and their setting, it is important to know how and why they came into being.

Dorothy Marguerite Callan Macardle was born in Dundalk, County Louth on March 8th, 1889. She was the eldest of five children. Her father, Thomas Callan Macardle, had built up several successful businesses, the most notable being the Macardle, Moore & Co. Brewery in Dundalk. Thomas Macardle was a Catholic and "Home Ruler"; a supporter of the Redmonite branch of the Irish Party, who accepted a knighthood for his services to business. His brother was the outspoken Jesuit priest, Father Andrew Macardle of St. Francis Xavier's in Upper Gardiner Street, Dublin.

Dorothy's mother, Lucy Ross, was an Anglican who had converted to Catholicism before she married Thomas Macardle in 1888. Dorothy had a background of wealth and privilege. Dorothy's three brothers were all sent to a Catholic boarding school—the famous Oratory School, long regarded as the Catholic Eton. Dorothy and her young sister, Mona, who became a stage actress, were sent to the Alexandra School, Dublin. Dorothy went on to take a first class honours degree in English and a Teacher's Training Diploma.

When John Redmond, Leader of the Irish Party, called for Irish nationalists to support Britain at the outbreak of the 1914-18 War, on the promise of "Home Rule" should Britain emerge victorious, two of Dorothy's brothers enlisted in the British Army. The third brother, Donald, was too young to join; he later became a stage and silent movie actor. Dorothy's favourite brother, Kenneth, was killed on the Somme in July 1916. A second brother, John, survived as a decorated war hero.

The year 1916 had a marked affect on Dorothy, as it had on many. She had witnessed the brutality with which the Dublin insurrection had been crushed. She changed her political position from being a "Home Ruler", like her father and brothers, to joining Sinn Féin after it became the voice of republicanism at its 1918 Ard Fheis. She was among the observers who attended the historic opening of the first Dáil, when Sinn Féin, having won 73 of the 105 parliamentary seats, met and declared unilateral declaration of independence.

The fact that her brother Kenneth had been killed actually hardened her republican viewpoint—that Ireland should be free to choose its own wars and not be coerced into any. According to one of her pupils, Lilian Dalton, the young man that Dorothy was to marry had been killed at Bouleaux Wood in September of 1916.

While remaining on the staff of Alexandra College, where she became Pfeiffer Professor of English, Dorothy did some clandestine work for the national movement, working with the White Cross and acting as an intermediary with Mrs. Margot Asquith, wife of the former Prime Minister, to see if a dialogue could be opened between the London and Dublin governments. She hardly spoke of her rôle during the War of Independence and only after her death did information emerge from the military archives.

Prior to this turbulent background, she had begun to contribute verse and articles to the Alexandra College magazine. She also edited several text books for Macmillan of London—commentaries on *Twelfth Night*, *The Tempest*, *Le Morte d'Arthur*, and Philip Sidney's *In Defence of Poesy*. Her first publicly performed play, *Asthara*, had been produced at the Little Theatre, Dublin, in 1918. This was followed by *Atonement* at the Abbey later that year. Her next play, *Ann Kavanagh*, was also produced at the Abbey by Lennox Robinson in May 1922. It was set against the 1798 uprising in Wexford.

Dorothy was beginning to gain a literary reputation when the Civil War broke out in June of 1922. When the Dáil narrowly split over the acceptance of a treaty with London, which set up a Free State under the Crown and partitioned Ireland, Dorothy committed herself to the republican anti-treaty side. She helped Erskine Childers edit *An Phoblacht*, travelling to Belfast where she witnessed the pogrom against Catholics. And when it was deemed wise for Childers to leave Dublin and join the anti-treaty forces in the south-west, she went with him as far as Waterford, so that as a couple they might not draw as much suspicion as would a single man travelling alone. Returning to Dublin, she became involved in the Women's Defence League, formed in August 1922. She also began to edit *Irish Freedom*, a journal dealing with the welfare of republican prisoners.

During this time she was staying in the house of her friend, the actress Maud Gonne MacBride, widow of Major John MacBride, an executed signatory of the 1916 Proclamation. This was at 73 St. Stephen's Green.

It was on Thursday, November 9th, 1922, that pro-treaty troops, then called the National Army (the Irish Free State did not come into being until December 6, 1922) raided the Sinn Féin offices at 23 Suffolk Street. Dorothy was arrested along with several others. It was a coincidence that Dorothy was at the Suffolk Street office that morning because she had gone there on an errand for Maud Gonne MacBride.

She was dismissed from her teaching position on November 16th, the week after her arrest. In her biography, *Dorothy Macardle: A Life*, Nadia Smith, speaking of Dorothy's father Thomas Macardle, claims: "Though concerned about her well-being, he felt a prison term would be beneficial for

Dorothy . . . " (40). However, the exchanges of letters from Thomas Macardle to Free State leaders, trying to secure Dorothy's release, tell an entirely different story.

Thomas Macardle first wrote to the secretary of William Cosgrave, President of the National Executive of the Free State Government, on December 19 complaining he had not been allowed to visit his daughter. On January 2 he was blandly informed "visits are not allowable". On January 9, he wrote again saying that he received a report from someone, recently released, saying "Dorothy is looking ill" and that "she is not sleeping". On January 13, Minister of Defence, Richard Mulcahy, made his position clear: "She refused to sign the Form of Undertaking" (not to criticise the Free State) "and in the circumstances, and in view of her previous record, it is not intended to release her".

Dorothy's mother, writing from Stanhope Court Hotel, South Kensington, London SW7, on January 17, pointed out her daughter, "against whom no charge has been made", was being imprisoned with "girls who are just following ideals". She suggests that she and Sir Thomas might persuade Dorothy, if released, to leave Ireland while the Civil War continued. Cosgrave informed her that "the matter is altogether in the hands of the Military Authorities". The campaign to get Dorothy released caused J. J. O'Neill of *The Manchester Guardian* to write to President Cosgrave on April 18, 1923, to the effect that, if Dorothy was released, she could be persuaded to leave Ireland by the offer of a job on *The Manchester Guardian* (now *The Guardian*).

Receiving no response from Mulcahy, Thomas Macardle secured appointments with Cosgrave no less than three times in one week. He also saw General Gearóid O'Sullivan, who gave Macardle some support. Mulcahy, however, was intractable. Dorothy actually wrote to him from prison on April 14 pointing out the cause for her imprisonment: "(a) that I am a writer (b) that I have refused to sign a certain form.—I am not aware that, even according to the Free State assumption of authority, either of these facts constitute a charge which could justify my detention". Thomas Macardle wrote a final letter to Richard Mulcahy pleading with him "to grant her immediate release". Mulcahy told Cosgrave that Dorothy was simply not going to be released. One could almost hear Thomas Macardle's despair when he wrote to President Cosgrave on April 30 exploding, "For God's sake do something."

When Cosgrave offered Thomas Macardle an appointment as a Senator in the Free State Senate, Macardle immediately refused, still disgusted by Dorothy's treatment.

By this time many of the women prisoners had gone on hunger strike. In January 1923, Dorothy had been transferred from Mountjoy to Kilmainham. Kilmainham was soon densely packed with women prisoners and the authorities decided to transfer some of them again. On April 30th, 1923, selected women were told by the prison governor that they would be removed to the military jail at the North Dublin Union. If they did not cooperate, they would be removed with force. Dorothy was one of them.

Dorothy's later account of seeing male CID men, brought in for the removal, beating up the female prisoners, makes for sickening reading. Some women had heart attacks during the beatings and one had her head smashed against the iron bars. Dorothy goes on: "Then my own turn came, after I had been dragged from the railings, a great hand closed on my face, blinding and stifling me, and thrust me down to the ground, among tramping feet. I heard someone who saw it scream . . . After that I remember being carried by two or three men and slung down in the surgery . . . " The prisoners were later thrown into lorries and taken to the Military Prison of the North Dublin Union.

Introduction

Whether Cosgrave did manage to over-rule Mulcahy, no documentation has yet been found. However, Dorothy was finally released on May 9, 1923. She brought out of her imprisonment a collection of short stories that she had written to pass the time.

Under the extreme conditions in which the prisoners were held—with even her own father's requests to visit her rejected—how did Dorothy get access to the means to write stories? The circumstances were told to me in June 1987 by Mrs. Lilian Soiron, then living in Dún Laoghaire. As Lilian Frances Dalton she had been one of Dorothy's pupils at Alexandra College. In 1922, at the age of eighteen years, Lilian had won the Pfeiffer English Prize at the time Dorothy was still Pfeifer Professor of English at the College. Dorothy had been admired and respected by her pupils and fellow staff. In school, she had never spoken of her political views. Therefore Lilian was shocked when she heard that Dorothy was incarcerated in Mountjoy.

A determined young woman, Lilian visited Dorothy at Mountjoy. Although her request to see her former teacher was refused, she was eventually able to supply her with paper and pens. She even sent in books, although Dorothy's request for a copy of Plato's *Republic* was returned with the word *Republic* scored out by the prison censor.

Lilian, who died on May 30th, 1997, became a translator from French, but can also add to her "literary fame" as being the person without whom the following short stories could not have been written. Lilian honoured me, not only with her reminiscences and surviving papers connected with Dorothy, but insisted on presenting me with a copy of *Earth-Bound*, signed and given to her by Dorothy at Christmas 1924.

Of the stories she had brought out of her prison cell, she began to place some in such publications as *The Dublin*

Magazine, *The Irish World*, *Éire*, *Sinn Féin*, *The Irish Nation*, and the US magazine *Columbia*. Nine of the stories were collected and published in volume form the following year, in December 1924, by Harrigan Press, Worcester, Massachusetts in the USA.

The stories Dorothy wrote in her cell were, perhaps naturally, set against the conflict in Ireland. They are also linked by the characters of Úna and Frank O'Carroll, who run a magazine called *Tri-Colour* in Philadelphia, and who provide a sympathetic ear to their republican visitors.

The tragedy of armed conflict and its individual effects is viscerally painted. The stories incorporate themes that intrigued her; themes out of the myths and legends of Ireland: ghostly interventions, dreams and premonitions, clairvoyance, and always the Otherworld in parallel with this one. It is so easy to dismiss them, as some have, merely as part of the narrative of "Irish nationalism" of the time, but the supernatural elements make them much more than that. It is true that the stories often do not have the polish of her later writing, but they have the essential ingredients that would develop into the mastery shown in her later novels.

For many years Dorothy had been fascinated by the Irish Literary Revival, the outpouring of non-fiction and fiction on Irish myths and legends. She loved the supernatural quality in folk stories and would later recall in a talk broadcast on Radio Éireann how she would listen to Maud Gonne telling stories about her personal clairvoyant experiences. "Madame would come upstairs to rest and drink cocoa beside my fire and would speak of her memories" ("They Say it Happened: Queer Stories for All Hallows", 31 October 1955).

For the stories that appeared in *Earth-Bound*, Dorothy used initials to dedicate each story to her fellow prisoners with the exception of two stories, which were dedicated to women writers who had influenced her writing and attitudes.

"Earth-Bound" has much of the quality of "spirit of place". Set in the Wicklow Hills in winter, two republican escapees during the War of Independence are surrounded by Black and Tans and are about to be discovered. When all is lost, the hunters are distracted and drawn off by a figure—but is it apparition or reality? One person thinks it is the ghost of the escaping "Red Hugh". One of Dorothy's favourite plays was "The Escape of Red Hugh" by Alice Milligan (1866-1953), first performed at the Abbey in 1900. It is significant that Dorothy dedicated the seventh story in this collection, "By God's Mercy", to "A.M."

"Earth-Bound" was written in Mountjoy towards the end of December 1922 when Dorothy found herself sharing a cell with the Waterford novelist Rosamund Jacob (1888-1960). It was to her, "R.J.", that Dorothy dedicated the story, which also appears to be her first written short story.

The theme of intervention from the Otherworld continues in "Samhain". The Celtic Samhain festival remains with us; more widely known as Hallowe'en, the eve of All Hallows' Day, which was the one night of the year when the Celtic Otherworld became visible to this one, and those who had been wronged could return to exact vengeance on the living. Dorothy has her own take on this and her setting is the time of the Great Hunger. She dedicated "Samhain" to "T.O'C.", Teresa O'Connell (1899-1998), a fellow prisoner and friend.

"The Brother", containing another ghostly intervention to save a life, was dedicated to "F.O'B.", fellow inmate Florence O'Byrne from Dublin. The fourth story, "The Prisoner", was inscribed to "E.C." in memory of a great influence in Dorothy's intellectual development—Ethna Carbery (1866-1911), a feminist, republican, poet, and short story writer. Here we find the shade of Lord Edward

Fitzgerald, the executed 1798 leader, still stalking Kilmainham Gaol. When the editor of *Éire* published the story under the title "The Prisoners (1798-1923)", Dorothy wrote a letter asking for a correction to her title as she felt it was misleading. Her story was set in the jail during the Black and Tan campaign.

"The Return of Niav" was dedicated to "L.S.", Lizzie (Essie) Snoddy. Lizzie was only sixteen years old when arrested. She was creative with her crochet and needlework and helped the women maintain their clothes, but is remembered for making a forbidden Irish tricolour flag for the prisoners.

"De Profundis" was dedicated to "L.O'B.", Lily O'Brennan (1878-1948), who had been arrested in Suffolk Street at the same time as Dorothy; she was also a writer of plays, short stories, and children's stories in both Irish and English. In "De Profundis" we have a "ghostly Mass", the redemption of a priest who had broken a sacred promise.

"The Portrait of Róisín Dhu" was dedicated to "S.H." another feminist republican and fellow prisoner, Sighle Humphreys (1899-1994). Like "The Return of Niav", this story is concerned with women's relationships with one another in a conflict situation.

"A Story Without an End", dedicated to "N.C.", was for Nora Connolly (1893-1981), the second daughter of James Connolly, the Irish Marxist leader and signatory of the 1916 Proclamation who was subsequently executed in Kilmainham. Nora had just married Seamus O'Brien, a fellow republican and socialist, who had also been imprisoned. She was to go on to write several books and serve three times in the Irish Senate. When Dorothy died, she remembered Nora in her will.

Several of the stories that Dorothy wrote in prison were not included in the 1924 volume, but they rightly take their place in this new edition. "Escape", published in *Sinn Féin*,

December 20, 1924; "The Venetian Mirror", from *Dublin Magazine*, November 1924; and two stories published in the American *Columbia* magazine, "The Curlew's Cry" and "The Black Banks", in June 1926 and January 1926, respectively. They, too, have that same supernatural intervention that Dorothy was fond of using to help her protagonists.

On her release from jail, Dorothy had no job. Sinn Féin offered her one as researcher for £2 10s a week. She involved herself in investigations on their behalf and her collection of articles on incidents during the Civil War in Kerry was collected in the booklet *The Tragedies of Kerry* (1924). The Free State government were forced to hold an inquiry, but this was under the control of Dorothy's *bête noir*, Richard Mulcahy, who dismissed the claims.

Dorothy soon became a power house of writing: investigative journalism, short stories, and new plays for the Abbey and the Gate. Through the 1930s she would also contribute talks and stories to Radio Éireann and, when the *Irish Press* was launched, became its leading theatre critic. She was first to notice the talent of a young Orson Welles making his first stage appearance. She also wrote political features and covered League of Nations meetings when Éamon de Valera was its president.

Dorothy became a founder member of de Valera's new republican party, Fianna Fáil, in 1926, and served as a member of its first National Executive Council. She had become a personal friend of de Valera and his wife Sinéad. It was not surprising, therefore, that when her seminal history of 1916-1923, *The Irish Republic*, was published in 1937, a frequently repeated claim was that Dorothy was "an apologist" for de Valera. She was not. De Valera wrote in his introduction: "Her interpretations and conclusions are her own. They do not represent the doctrine of any party. In many cases they are not in accord with my views . . ."

In fact, from 1935, Dorothy had begun to grow apart from Fianna Fáil. That year de Valera proposed his new constitution, demoting the rôle of women and giving special recognition to the Catholic Church. During the referendum on the proposed constitution, Dorothy publicly argued that women had fared better under the 1922 Free State constitution. When the 1937 Constitution came into law she was the driving force behind a new political party— The Women's Social & Political League—becoming its first president on November 25, 1937. This "women's rights party", as it was called, put up candidates for the Dáil in 1938 and 1943.

Another important difference between Dorothy and de Valera was the latter's neutrality policy in 1939. Dorothy had been a long-time anti-Fascist, both during the Spanish Civil War and through the rise of the Third Reich. "Hitler's War is everyone's war," she declared. In 1940, returning from a trip to the USA, where she had spoken in support of civil rights for African-Americans, and was awarded an honorary doctorate, she decided to move to London. She declared her support for the Allies, broadcasting for the BBC and for American radio while continuing her own literary output. It was in London that she wrote three of her supernatural-themed novels. *The Uninvited* (1941; originally titled *Uneasy Freehold*) and *The Seed Was Kind* (1944); then *Fantastic Summer*, re-titled as *The Unforeseen* (1946) and adapted on BBC Television in 1955. Her last novel, *Dark Enchantment* (1953), was written after she returned to Ireland at the end of the war.

As a "neutral" Irish citizen Dorothy was able to specialise in the problems of refugees across war-torn Europe, and her second major non-fiction work became *The Children of Europe* (Gollancz, 1947). Today we might still learn much from her work on refugee experiences and problems. Once more Dorothy was reticent about the rôle she played at this period. But in 1946 Robert Briscoe TD paid tribute to her in the Dáil, commenting on the debt that the Irish Government owed her for the information she had been able to pass on about conditions in Europe.

After the war, she returned to Ireland and bought a house at Howth. She continued to broadcast, write stories, articles, plays, and even a twelve part radio serial "The Shadow of the Glens".

Dorothy Macardle died in a hospital in Drogheda on December 23, 1958. Her last non-fiction book was published posthumously. It was on one of her favourite subjects—*Shakespeare: Man and Boy* (Faber, 1961).

She was buried in St. Fintan's, Howth, at a service attended by President Seán T. O'Kelly, Taoiseach Éamon de Valera, and official representatives from all the parties in the Dáil and Senate. While the politicians rightly paid tribute to her political works and activities, sadly, no one seemed to mention that she also deserves a niche in literary Valhalla as the author of one of the classic ghost stories of all time. That apart, Dorothy Macardle deserves that recognition for all her work and, for that omission, this volume is a respectful tribute.

Peter Berresford Ellis
October 2015

Captivity

Out on the high road in the sun
They walk whose souls are dark with shame,
Fettered and bowed with heavy fear,
Who dare not speak the glorious name
They swore to die for, yester-year,
For faith is broken, hope undone.

Free hearts that never break their troth,
And unsurrendered spirits, we
Look out on the eternal stars
And take again proud freedom's oath
Unshamed, and know the prison bars,
But symbols of our liberty.

Kilmainham.

Earth-Bound

(FOR R.J.)

"Do you think that people who are not Irish know what home-sickness is?" Úna said.

"It is harder being away from a country that is in trouble," Michael O'Clery answered, "than from a country that is at peace. It is not home-sickness only—it is that you want to be in the fight."

He spoke contentedly. It was his last night in Philadelphia; tomorrow he was going home.

Úna's pale little face looked sad in the dying fire-light; the coming and going of Irish friends filled her, always, with joy and pain. Even Frank's keen face grew wistful and, for myself, an unbearable pang of "*heim-weh*" silenced me.

Úna spoke again, after a pause.

"Do you know what I miss more than the people, more than the dear places?" she said. "It is that sense one has everywhere in Ireland—in the glens, and in Dublin—the old squares on the north side, and the quays—of the companionship of the dead."

Frank laughed in brotherly mockery.

"They stay in Ireland, I suppose, sooner than go to Heaven? Or is it doomed to it they are, instead of Hell?"

But Michael said seriously, "I believe she's right."

Michael had something to tell us: that could be felt. It was past midnight but Úna put coal on the fire.

1

Three weeks ago Michael had arrived, without a passport, in Philadelphia, on some mission not to be disclosed, and, like most friendly travellers from Ireland had found his way soon to the young editors of the *Tri-Colour*, Úna and Frank O'Carroll. Within their hospitable studio his few idle hours were spent.

Nowhere outside Dublin have I known so shabby yet lovable a room. It was perhaps their one treasure, Hugo Blake's glorious "Dawn", that made one seem to breathe there the air of home. That picture is magical. There is nothing painted but the hills of Clare-Galway seen from the water and daybreak in the sky behind, yet it is the dawn of all that Ireland has been waiting for these seven hundred years.

"You could go away from that picture," Michael said once, "and die."

There was little else—brown walls, three uncurtained windows looking down on the Square, at evening all blue shadow and amber lights; faded draperies on the divans and many-coloured cushions around the fire; it was enough, with Frank's iridescent, satirical humour and Úna's pleasure in her friends, to create an illusion inexpressibly restful. It was the exiles' oasis of living waters at the end of each arid week.

It was late at night, as now, when all but a guest or two had gone, that the talk would grow full of reminiscences and omens and prophesies and dreams, and strange adventures would be told.

Not one word had Michael said, yet, of the perils that followed his escape, but Úna's remark had started some deep train of thought in him. He repeated, in a tone of deep conviction:

"I believe she's right."

"You think they stay—?" I asked.

"Some," he replied. "Some that died for Ireland, thinking more of Ireland than Heaven at the end."

"And they're wanted," he added gravely. "They are surely wanted still."

"Do you know Glenmalure?" he asked then.

I knew it, a deep valley of the Wicklow hills, shut out from life, compelling mournful thoughts.

"They might well be there," I said.

"I'll tell you a thing happened there," Michael went on, "and you can explain it the way you please. It's there Donal and I were on our keeping after we escaped from Mountjoy."

"Donal O'Donel?" asked Frank.

"Yes; he got a life-sentence, you know, and we were to be transferred to Pentonville. My own sentence was only two years, but I was fairly desperate for him. If you ever knew him you'd understand; he'd never been in a city a week together—a long-limbed mountainy lad, the quickest brain I ever met, extraordinarily confident and proud. He'd a kind of thirst for life for its own sake that you don't find often among the boys, yet the death-sentence seemed to give him a kind of joy; 'twas the commutation he couldn't stand—things looked fairly hopeless, you know, then—and Pentonville for life.

"We knew 'twould be a desperate chance; he had a damaged foot, he'd be hard to disguise too, with his fiery hair; but 'twas worth any risk and we had Pierce O'Donovan outside—the gaol was never built Pierce couldn't break; we made a plan you'd think crazy and got away.

"I'll not forget that night—the sky over us and a grand wind full of rain and a cruel moon and we driving like fury in an open car, clean through the city and over the hills! Half a dozen times we were halted, but Pierce had licences and all and we got through. He put us with an old couple in the last cottage in the glen—Glenmalure—who welcomed us like their own. We were to stay there till Donal's foot would be well, then we'd be sent for to join the column in the hills.

" 'Twas a strange land to us both—different altogether from Sligo or Donal's place, Donegal: a steep narrow valley in a wilderness of naked hills, all rocks, bracken and dead gorse, treacherous with spots of bog; the hills are channelled everywhere with torrents—you hear the noise of them night and day. Old Moran was forever warning us: 'Many a one got lost here and was never found; the Glen doesn't like strangers,' he used to say.

"I had no love for the Glen; 'twould be beautiful on the frosty mornings when Lugnacullia had a crest of snow, but in the afternoons—'twas December—when the sun fell behind Clohernagh and the whole place went chill and dark under a vast shadow, you felt drowned . . . I said to Donal it was too like Synge's play. Donal didn't know Synge's play; he never had much use for books; he'd rather be making history than reading it; he loved the Glen: ' 'Tis a grand place,' he said, 'heroic; it remembers the old times.'

"His foot was better; he could hobble a good way with a stick and we explored the nearer hills on those bright cold mornings—Slieve Moan and Fananieran and Cullentragh. Donal was wild to climb to the Three Lochs, but old Moran made a scare: 'There are bog holes you'd sink in and never rise,' he said; ' 'twould be a good man would do it on a summer day, let alone in the snow'; and not a soul in the valley would guide us, so we gave it up.

"One day, though, we followed the torrent to Art's Loch; it was the longest climb Donal had done and he was pleased; a place like that exhilarated him. The sun was setting and there was a red stormy light on the water lying lost there in its hollow among the great hills. Dead solitary the loch is; I thought there was no life in it at all, but Donal was excited: ' 'Tis these places are haunted,' he said, 'by the old Chieftains and Kings.' He looked like one of them himself standing there with the ruddy light on his face; predestined to victory he looked. A song Mrs. Moran used to be quoting came into my head, about 'The King of Ireland's son' and 'the crown of his red-gold hair', but the sun sank and the shadow rose over him and a black thought crossed my mind—'He is the sort England always kills.' That place would make you afraid of death.

"There was trouble in the glens, we heard; it would likely be after Christmas before anyone would come for us; being ignorant of the country it would be useless setting off by ourselves. We got impatient waiting; maybe we went too freely about the hills; Donal was very heedless with strangers; they'd often stare at him as if wanting to remember his face. Anyway, on Christmas Eve the waiting came to an end.

" 'Twas a savagely cold day with a wind out of the north and a black sky and folks were staying at home. We sat all the evening with the Morans round a gorgeous fire talking, or rather listening to Donal's talk. He was in one of his keen, inventive moods when he'd plan laws and constitutions and lay out the whole government of Ireland the way you'd tell faery tales to a child. Some of his ideas would startle you, but he'd not let you off till you saw they were sound. He drew a map of Ireland on the bellows with a burnt stick and started planning a military defence; it was a great plan surely that he made. 'We could face the nations of the world,' he said, 'if we had no traitors in our own. Ireland's a natural fortress, the best God made.'

" 'God keep you!' said Mrs. Moran fervently: 'God spare you, son!'

"There was a sharp knock at the door and we stood up; old Moran opened; it was a girl, a neighbour's girl, who worked at the hotel; she was wet and breathless and shivering with cold. The Black and Tans were drinking at the hotel; they had raided Glendaloch and Laragh; they were raiding Glenmalure, 'For the two lads escaped out of Mountjoy.' She had guessed suddenly and deserted her work to warn us—run all the way. 'Beasts and devils they are! My God! if you heard the threats and curses! Into the hills with you,' she pleaded, 'for God's sake!'

"Donal looked at old Moran, 'Where will we go?' The old man shook his head wretchedly: 'If I could tell you that—'

" 'If you could get to Reilly's at the Three Lochs,' the girl said, 'they'll not look as far as that; or O'Toole's of Granabeg, or Mr. Barton's; but you'll not get so far; you'd have to pass Glendaloch.'

"Mrs. Moran was parcelling up food and sobbing, 'My God! My God! the boggy hills and the snow, and he with a broken foot!' Snow was falling, steady and deliberate, out of the leaden sky; Donal looked at it and smiled, the way you'd smile at an enemy; it was better than Pentonville. We thanked brave little Nannie and hugged poor old Mrs. Moran and set out, facing north.

"There was the ford to cross, then the precipitous face of Lugduff Mountain to scale; by the time we had clambered to the ridge and looked down on Glenmalure again it was night. We saw through the snowfall white lights rushing along the road below, and shots sounding like volleys echoed among the hills.

"Our way lay over a rugged moorland, unbroken save for boulders and thwarted trees, a waste of bog and heather, stiff grasses and withered bracken all buried in snow; no light or outline of a house was visible; only the curves of the hilltops against the sky. We knew nothing of these regions; nothing of the direction in which any habitation lay; we could only push straight onward and trust to luck, keeping our faces to the wind.

"But there was no luck with us; the snow never ceased falling; not one star shone; each step was a separate labour; the snow drove in our faces; I grew heavy and numb with cold; Donal dragged forward steadily with the help of his stick, but he did not speak at all; I saw his face by the pale gleam of the snow; it was white and grim with pain. He refused angrily to take my arm.

"It comes back like a nightmare now: the two of us plodding on towards nothing, labouring up hill and down again, hour after painful hour, the desert around us looking forever the same; we might have been walking in a circle for all I knew. At last Donal reeled and clutched my arm, then stood up, breathing through his teeth. I asked if his foot had given out. 'If I could rest it a minute,' he gasped; 'it's only the lumpy ground . . .'

"The snow had lightened a little and we could see: a black heaven and a white earth; sharp granite edges thrusting up through the snow; down hill, to our left, a clump of trees.

"My own feet were like lead, frozen: I was stupefied with cold and could think of nothing to do; I felt a monstrous weight was against us, compassing our destruction: the hills were malignant to us, and the wind, and God. Donal had his senses still; he whispered, 'Make for the trees!'

"We reached the clump of firs at last and got a respite from the wind; Donal sank down on a fallen trunk, easing the tortured foot; I leaned against a tree, dizzy; I was afraid to sit down. Already that craving was over me that comes so fatally in snow, to abandon the forlorn, dreamlike struggle and lie down in the soft fleeciness and sleep. But Donal had risen, suddenly, as though called: 'Come on,' he said tensely, 'we mustn't rest.'

"We stood together in the open again, wondering which way to go; one way seemed as meaningless as another; allied to the same end. Donal looked at me for a moment remorsefully: 'I'm sorry, Mike,' he said, 'you could have managed it alone.'

"I was answering angrily, but he stopped me with 'Hush! Look there!' pointing straight in front of him; then he started forward again whispering, 'Come on!'

"He was following something; I followed him and at last, through the veil of blowing snow, I saw it too—a tall, dark, striding form.

"A crazy zig-zag course we made, following that far-off figure which never noticed us, never beckoned us, never turned.

"Down a steep rough hillside we went and far along the bank of a frozen stream; up a wooded slope and out once more on a white plain. Dizzied with swirling snow, choked and aching with the cold, we followed—no thought or will left to us of our own.

"Donal stopped short now and then for a moment, paralysed by pain, but limped on again; our guide never stopped; we never came near enough to call to him, never near enough to see more than the lithe, tall figure of a boy moving fearlessly through the night.

"We were travelling over a difficult, stony hillside, steering towards a black grove of trees, when Donal lurched sideways and leaned on my shoulder, his eyes closed. I saw he was done, exhausted, and I held him, looking for our guide. He had gone; he seemed to have disappeared into the trees. But below us lay the road: it would be easier going; it must lead to houses: hope—the hope of dear life—rose up in me, and Donal opened his eyes. 'Come on,' he said faintly, standing up and then, with a twisted smile, 'I'll have to lean on you.'

"We had not gone ten yards when the air rumbled with a familiar sound and below us from the right, round the turn of the hill they came driving—those lurching, malignant lights. We were in full view from the road, on the bare hillside, and those were lorries below.

"I saw them crashing along and stopping, saw the rutty road splashed with brilliance from the headlights; saw the men dismounting and heard a hoarse voice shouting orders as they scattered to left and right.

"I looked at Donal. 'Run,' he commanded, 'I'll follow,' and at the first step he pitched headlong and lay on the snow.

"On the hillside opposite, the far side of the road, a searchlight from the lorry began to play. To rise, to attempt to drag or carry Donal would have betrayed us both; he was in a dead faint, his face like marble; I lay down, crouched over him in the snow.

"Men out of the lorries came swarming up, searching with flash lamps, cursing brutally as they came. Then the searchlight swung over and began to play along our side of the hill. The broad beam came creeping over the slope: I saw the intense black and white pictures leap out of the darkness one by one—saw every boulder, every bunch of stubble as it swept steadily towards where we lay. The searchers crossed it, reeling—they were drunk; they carried bayonets; they were Black and Tans. I pulled my gun out and held it at Donal's head—I meant to fire when the light touched us—God forgive me! what else was there to do?

"Then, suddenly, I saw our guide again; down from the cover of the trees he came leaping, between us and the path of light. I heard the triumphant yell of the searchers as the beam caught him full—a tall slim figure with lifted arms. He stood an instant, then ran, swift as a deer, clean across the shaft of light, away from us into the dark again; volleys of shots and a wild clamour of yells followed him as he ran.

"I staggered to my feet, dazed, half-believing I was in a dream; for I had seen him when the light fell on him—the long limbs and the high head and the red wind-blown hair; I would have sworn a hundred oaths that it was Donal, but Donal lay beside me on the snow.

"The shouts and firing followed the flyer and the sweeping light followed him over the hill. The lorries were turned and followed, driven madly along the road, and we were left in the empty night. I put my coat over him, chafed his hands and tried to warm his lips with my breath—nothing seemed any good. An awful memory came to me of the story of poor Art O'Neill, fugitive in those glens, frozen to death.

"I began to run blindly, for no reason, towards the trees.

"Out of the grove of trees a light shone; it was shining from an open door. I stumbled into the light and up the steps of a stone house; a grey-haired man stood there and a girl. 'There's a man out there,' I told them, 'in the snow.'

"They called servants and ran out with lanterns and a great dog followed them and found him and they brought him in.

"It took a long time to revive him, and his foot was lamed with frost-bite, but not much, and, but for that, he was soon well.

"We had come, I think, to the kindest folk in Ireland—the O'Byrnes of Glendasan. We must have travelled a dangerous way, they said, through Glenrigh, where King O'Toole is buried, past the grave of poor Art O'Neill—they knew the whole region—it was their own, and its histories, but they knew nothing about our guide.

"The Black and Tans caught nobody in the Glen."

Amazed faces were turned to Michael as he ended his tale. Frank O'Carroll frowned but was silent; Max Barry, who is a rapacious historian, spoke eagerly: "Art O'Neill? . . . Glenmalure! . . . Didn't Aodh Ruadh . . . wasn't it there?"

"Yes," Úna answered with glowing eyes, "Aodh Ruadh O'Donal!—Red Hugh!"

Michael nodded, "That is what Donal says."

Mountjoy.

10

Samhain

(FOR T. O'C.)

It was only on rare and premeditated occasions that the studio was visited by Úna's old friend Andrew FitzGerald. He had been burrowing through his great work on Celtic Etymology for so many years that "by the law of inertia," he said, he could not stop. But once or twice in a season he would emerge, blinking, into the light and visit his young friends. He came one April evening to meet Doctor Christiansen, the Norwegian folklorist, and he was as happy as a Leprechaun talking of trolls and pooka and the Sídhe and Norse monuments in Ireland and the ship symbol in Brúgh-na-Bóinne.

Doctor Christiansen had been exploring the Gaeltacht and was full of delight in the people he had met.

"What is to me most charming," he said, "is their good friendship with their dead. I hoped much to meet a revenant, or a woman of the Sídhe—but alas, to a Norseman, she would not appear!"

Úna looked at him reproachfully. "You are laughing at us," she said.

"Indeed no!" he replied quickly. "I have learned so much, I no longer venture to disbelieve. To me, magics and religions all are one, and all very full with what is true. And those people—they speak in good faith. It was in Kerry, more than anywhere in the world," he went on, "that poor, beautiful country, that they told me mysteries of the dead."

"Still, you thought the people credulous," FitzGerald said gently; "but you will not suspect a lexicographer of being fantastical. I, too, could tell you of strange happenings in Kerry—a mystery of the dead."

"Daddy Fitz!" Frank exclaimed, "how well you never told us you had seen a ghost!"

"But I saw no ghost, Avic," he replied, his crumpled old face sweet with a reminiscent smile. "If I had seen him, I think, truly, I should now be far away. I will tell you, if you like, what I heard."

"If you please!" begged Dr. Christiansen eagerly.

"Please!" said Úna. "Was it long ago?"

"Long ago indeed—when I was young. I was learning Irish at that time and I went to live in a small fishing village in West Kerry where the people had the language still—and had very little else.

"I made the best friend of my life there; 'twas Father Patrick O'Rahilly, the parish priest, a middle-aged man, but white-haired, very delicate—the nearest creature to a saint I have ever known.

"No life could be more lonely, I suppose, than that of an Irish priest in those desert regions of the west and south. This man had been a student and traveller in his youth—he had a very subtle, originating mind—and there he was, marooned among the poorest fisher-folk in existence—too poor himself to buy books. My coming, heretic though he found me—I was a sort of agnostic then—was a godsend to him; he made no secret of it from the first, and I was as welcome to the Presbytery as if it had been my home.

"I rejoiced in the man and in his queer, desultory house; there was charm, life about it, though 'twas not old. It had been built a generation ago by a Father Howe. He had chosen the site for the sake of the grand view. Over Dingle Bay, you looked, through a gap in the trees, across to the mountains—mountains like mother-o'-pearl. To secure that he did what the folk said was a wrongful thing; he built on an old pathway that ran from the chapel to the ancient graveyard on the hill. That path had been disused altogether since the opening of the military road. He harmed no living soul, building on it; moreover he lived jovially, and died piously in his bed; all the same the people never gave up blaming his choice. ' 'Twas bad,' they said, 'to go meddling with an old path; there's them might be wishful to be using it still.'

"There was one old woman who used to beg Father Patrick with tears in her eyes, every time she met him, to take a house somewhere else. I remember the day his patience gave out.

" 'Maura O'Shea,' he said sternly, 'are you suggesting that a priest of God has cause to dread the vengeance of the living or of the dead?'

"And 'Ah, Father Patrick, dear,' she replied in distress, 'don't you know we'd stay out of Heaven itself, and Saint Peter bidding us step in, to do a good turn to you, alive or dead?'

"They are people who know how to love and to speak out of the heart as well as out of the mind.

"My coming brought the bad luck, so it seemed. All that Summer and Autumn one disaster after another broke on those unfortunate people, until, towards Samhain time, the last blow came—Father Patrick fell ill."

"Sah-wen?" Max repeated enquiringly. His tongue tangled always over Irish words. Dr. Christiansen looked up, smiling:

"Your Festival of the Dead?"

"It corresponds, doesn't it, to the Feast of Balor?" FitzGerald went on: "Mananaan, the god of the under-world was potent then and it is a time of strange happenings in Gaelic countries still. It is then, in Ireland, that the living pray for the dead, invoking the prayers of the holy saints; it is then, old people will tell you, that the drowned come up out of the sea—they come to draw away living souls; there are footfalls you must not follow, knocking to which you dare not open; dead voices call . . .

"The trouble began about July; 'twas the wettest July Corney O'Grady remembered, and he was ninety-five years old.

"August was a month of storm; day after day passed and the little boats dared not venture out, while the pirating French trawlers, hardier vessels, came plundering the spawn-beds—destroying the harvest of the sea. The farms, no more than potato patches among the stones, which were the fisher-folks' last resource, failed them, too; the potatoes came black and rotten from the summer rains.

"It was one of those seasons of heart-breaking tragedy which are recurrent on those Irish coasts where the people dwell in the Valley of the Shadow all their lives. By the end of summer the spectre of famine had come.

"I think that but for Father Patrick many of those poor souls would have boarded up their windows, as in the old days, and lain down in their bare huts to die; but he was with them like an inspired and inspiring spirit, giving them courage, energy and hope. He got an instructress from Cork to start a knitting industry and the girls worked hard, but they could get no price for the garments they made. And all the time the sky was pitiless. 'You'd think' old Corney, said bitterly, 'God grudged Ireland the light of the sun.'

"The men began to get desperate. They saw the children growing wizened and sickly before their eyes. They were without milk, without flour, without even Indian meal. I don't think they cried or complained, the children, but they had not the strength to climb the steep road to the school. You'd see them creeping among the potato ridges, turning over the sods, in the hope that a good potato might remain.

14

"The men took to going out in any weather at all—going twenty miles out to sea in their canoes, and they'd come home without having netted a fish. Many a time, at the pleading of a distracted wife or mother, Father Patrick went down to them to protest, but even he could not hold them now. 'Sure, Father,' they would answer, 'there is death only before us anyway, and isn't it better go look for it on the water than bide waiting it on the black land? What good are we to the childer, and we walking the roads?'

"The best boat in the village was owned by a grand old fellow named MacCarthy, his two sons and his son-in-law, Dermot Roche. There was a tribe of young children dependent on this crew, and I watched the demons of misery give place to the demons of recklessness in the sombre eyes of the men.

"I troubled most about Dermot. The man attracted me strongly and had taken me under his protection from the first. He was a creature of fierce attachments; he loved me, I think, for my love of the Irish; he never let a word of English across his tongue. To my imagination he incarnated the spirit of that savage, primitive, gentle place; hard and gaunt he was as the rocks, protective as the hills; he seemed to know its terrible history 'in his bones'. I never saw him smile, but I have seen him glow with a kind of angry joy. He used to take me out fishing in the early morning to teach me the old ranns and proverbs that he knew I loved, and he would sing to me on the water wild old traditional songs in a rich voice that had a drone in it like the wind. He had a shy, smiling little wife, and half-a-dozen black-haired youngsters who seemed to live like sea-creatures among the rocks. Father Patrick had been good to the children, and for Father Patrick, Dermot would have faced the legions of Hell. In those famine days the man's face became terrible; his wife was expecting another child.

"I was sitting at the round table in the Presbytery, that black September evening, reading with Father Patrick the ancient annals which were his delight and mine, when Dermot unlatched the door and came striding in—a man angry with his God. Father Patrick's gentle welcome was too much for him; he sat down and laid his head on the table and wept. Annie had given birth to a seventh child and died.

"Father Patrick asked me to stay in the house in case any call should come, and went down with Dermot. He came back in the morning worn out, his habitual tranquillity gone.

" 'The men are losing hold of themselves,' he said. ' 'Tis not right. Dermot's left the neighbours to wake Annie, and gone off with MacCarthy in the boat.'

"All that day a diabolical gale was raging. The boat did not come home. By dusk the people were huddling together, silent and ghastly, at the little pier; as long as daylight lasted there was nothing visible but the grey, murderous sea. At dawn they launched the life-boat and it came back at noon. Mat Kearney climbed out of it and passed up through the crowd. He answered me with a heavy gesture of his hand: 'They're all away.' His own son was in it—one of the crew of eight. They had found the boat upside down.

"If Father Patrick had laboured before, he laboured after this like forty men; day and night, in wind and wet, he was in and out of the broken hovels, bringing what comfort there was to bring to forlorn old mothers and derelict young widows and starving families that had no man.

"I sent an appeal to the Dublin press and to friends in Boston which brought us enough to keep Dermot's orphans and the MacCarthy's for a few weeks; after that, neighbours who had forgotten what it was not to be hungry took the children to their own homes.

"Our language studies were all laid aside. When Father Patrick was not visiting he would be brooding and writing and calculating, trying to work out schemes. He knew little of the commercial world and I thought most of his suggestions impracticable; but one seemed sound. He began corresponding with traders in Cork and Dublin, trying to work up a market for carrigeen moss—a kind of edible seaweed which grows in the rock pools and can be gathered at low tide. He hoped to have a sale for it very soon. It could never, of course, bring in much to the poor creatures, but the work and planning kept them from black despair.

"But all the time Father Patrick was struggling against illness, himself obsessed by a fear of breaking down. His people had no one else.

"Then, near and far along the coast, washed up by the tide, the bodies of the drowned fishermen came in. One by one we laid them with the multitude of their fathers, sea-faring generations, in the wind-swept graveyard beyond the house. And from each burial Father Patrick came home bowed as though under another load of care. Grief weakened him no less than the endless toil. I would have given all I had to take him away from it, to the South.

"It was on the evening we buried Dermot that the sickness came. I found him huddled in the chair in his parlour, unable to speak or move. His old housekeeper and I helped him upstairs and put him to bed and carried the red sods up to his room.

"The doctor had to ride out to us over Brandon Mountain. It was that dreaded scourge of the poor, typhoid; a desperate attack. Every day for a week he came, and he and Brigid and I were fighting avenging nature for that dear life. On the last day of October he told me there was no more hope and that I should send for the priest. I went down the village street with him, looking for a boy to ride out with the message; the men were at the street corners, the women at their doors, waiting, dumbly, for the doctor's

17

word. 'Pray for him; pray for him!' was all he said. I heard men sobbing as they turned away.

"Late in the evening the young priest came and gave the Viaticum to my dying friend. When he had gone and I went in to Father Patrick I found him lying very quiet with a happy radiance on his face. He held out his hand for mine. 'Stay by me tonight, Andreas,' he whispered. ' 'Twould be good to have you near when I set out.'

"You can imagine I felt desolate enough. For months this man had made the whole kindness of my world; I knew I'd never see his like again. And I had no resource. Bitterly I envied the good Catholic people with their boundless faith in prayer. They were praying for him that night, I knew well, in every cottage, and invoking prayers more powerful than their own—All Saints'—all Souls.

"When I drew the curtains and lit the lamp at nightfall he asked was it Samhain night. 'It is,' I answered, and he sighed distressfully: 'I ought to be praying for the dead.'

"There was a little oratory behind the bed-room where he used sometimes to say Mass. 'Would you light the altar candles for me, Andreas?' he said. 'That way they'll know I didn't forget . . . '

"I lit a candle and walking down the draughty passage, opened the oratory door. It was a bare little room with no adornment; there were only a few benches and the altar with its Tabernacle, four brass candle-sticks and white cloth, but it was full, to my imagination, of rest. I lit the candles and then, surrendering to a sudden whim, it may be of faith, I prayed. I suppose it was a pagan sort of prayer.

"When I went back to Father Patrick his eyes were closed and his breathing was so faint that I thought he had died, until I saw his fingers move feebly along his rosary beads.

"There was nothing that I could do but sit up the old chair by the fire putting fresh sods on from time to time, giving him a drink when I saw that he was awake. About midnight he began moaning; his face had grown grey and wan, and his fingers were groping about the quilt. I could see that he was in high fever. 'What will they do at all?' he kept murmuring unhappily, and 'I ought to be praying for the dead . . . ' Then: 'Pray that I'll be spared to them awhile, Andreas;' and again, moaning: 'God pity him, he can't pray!'

"I knew that he could scarcely live till dawn. Then the trance-like silence fell again, broken only by the long, wailing gusts of a wind that seemed to blow out of infinity and into infinity again, like a human soul.

"We forget, thank God, those intensities of desolation. I only know that the sense of Eternity, always appalling, fell on me in that quiet room—and, to me, Eternity was a void. The weak, insane moment in which I had prayed was over . . . the bright flame that had been my friend's spirit was going out . . . after life there was only the Abyss . . . and I could not hold him back; I knew no way . . .

"It was an hour or two after midnight, I suppose, when I roused myself and drank some black coffee and went over to my patient to see whether he slept.

"He was awake; his eyes were open; he was listening—listening to something which I did not hear. He did not look up at me or speak or move.

"I stood, wondering, beside the bed, and presently a sound came to my ears—faintly—a low, rhythmic murmur, like a multitude of voices at prayer. I listened and gradually I heard clearly, much more clearly—a soothing and entrancing sound. It came from the room behind the bedroom—the oratory. I leaned, listening, against the wall. It was prayer; I heard the prayers and responses—but not in Latin—it was Irish—I knew the soft, rich sounds.

"I suppose the language was my only passion—maybe I loved it better, even, than my friend; anyhow, in the mere joy and wonder of hearing it I became oblivious of everything else. Soon every syllable came to me, full and clear; I heard a long unfamiliar litany, full of noble phrases and ancient names—'Naov Finghin . . . Naov Breandan . . . Naov Colmcille . . . ' and, after the litany, prayers, long and ceremonious—the whole Mass.

While it lasted I stood spellbound, but when silence came I felt shaken with awful fear; I knelt down, suddenly, by the bed and stared at Father Patrick's face. His eyes were wide open; his lips were moving in quiet prayer; the flush of fever had gone; he seemed to have forgotten me; he said 'Amen!'

"From the oratory too, I heard a long 'Amen', like a contented sigh. I heard the sound of people rising from their knees, and their footsteps, soft and light, as of an innumerable multitude, went past the door. I heard them after a moment on the gravel outside, and low voices began caoining mournfully until a man's voice called quietly, '*Ná bí ag caoineadh anois*'—'Do not be caoining now!' That voice was strangely familiar; caught by it, as one's whole being may be caught by intolerable agony or joy, I waited, in a kind of rigour, for it to come again. I heard it, then—calling my own name, strongly and insistently, three times.

"I would have risen; I would have opened the door and rushed out, but Father Patrick's arm was around me, his hand pressed over my mouth. 'Don't answer,' he whispered urgently, and held me until the noises had passed away.

"He lay back on his pillow then, and smiled at me happily, and fell asleep."

FitzGerald, too, smiled happily as he ended his tale. He was tired. Doctor Christiansen's blue eyes were alight. "It was poor Dermot," he asked gently—"He who called?"

FitzGerald answered, "It was his voice."

"He would have loved to take you, instead of that other? If you had answered—is it not so—you would have followed within a year?"

"So Father Patrick said."

"And he recovered—your good friend?"

"Thank God," FitzGerald answered, "he is living still."

Doctor Christiansen spoke wonderingly, "They prayed for him well, those Dead."

Mountjoy.

The Brother
(FOR F. O'B.)

The news of the murder of Pierce O'Donovan at the height of Ireland's need of him was the worst of many bitter tidings that came to us that Spring. Frank and Úna half broke their hearts over it; they had loved that brilliant and happy-spirited man.

It was about four months later that Úna received a message from Dublin asking her hospitality for Pierce's young brother Larry who had been rescued from the hospital, where he was being doctored for the gallows, just in time.

He arrived in Philadelphia, a merry, though disabled wreck, in May, and revelled in the friendly atmosphere of Úna's home. He was not fretting, although Pierce had been hero and leader to him, brother and friend; he loved to talk about him as we loved to hear. His own fame—marvellous stories of Larry's exploits had preceded him—he regarded with amusement; he had got the credit, he said, for the work of a better man;—as to the tale of how he had dealt with three of the enemy single-handed—"I'll tell you the true story some day," he said, "and you'll see I was not so single-handed as they say." But it was not until his last night in Philadelphia that it was told—the story of Pierce O'Donovan's last great plan.

"If there was work Pierce was proud of," he said, " 'twas not his engineering stunts at all, but the gaol-breaking."

We knew that no prison had ever held Pierce longer than six weeks, and the stories of the rescues he effected from outside formed a mythological cycle—"At least two-thirds of it," Larry told us, "is true."

"But there never was anything he set out on with such mortal determination as the last—the capture of Kilbride Prison. Tyrrell was in it at the time you know, and Dick Brennan and MacNeill—eight altogether, the very best, to be hanged in the first week of March, and over five hundred unsentenced men.

"You know the way he could stir people up! He got Headquarters as keen on it as himself; they let him take all the men he wanted, and drop all other work; they gave him a free hand.

" 'Twas something like generalship, that plan! And the fine secrecy of it all! He had one man only inside, Tracy, a great fellow; he got into the night guard. Tyrrell was to get a short tunnel dug—forty feet—from the inside. All the rest Pierce was to do from outside, scientifically, with machines.

"He took three big houses in a row a good way from the prison and in a couple of weeks they were honey-combed with secret rooms and stuffed to bursting with explosives and guns. But when a raid came, in the thick of it, all they saw was a bead factory. Pierce was an expert at plaiting wire!

"The men he put on the job were mad on it; the work never stopped, night or day, and as the tunnel grew his idea grew; at first it was a rescue only he'd planned, but before the end 'twas the biggest thing ever tried.

"It was to come off on the First of March at night. The tunnel was double, you know. First Ryan, with about twenty, was to get in with guns, Tracy to unlock the doors, the prisoners to arm themselves and overpower the guard while the sentenced men were got away. Then the rush out of the prisoners by one tunnel, the rush in of our fellows with guns and mines—then the fight! An attack from outside, of course, at the same time. And when all was clear the grand old fortress to be blown sky-high!

"Pierce had the position and strength for every mine mapped down—there'd not be two stones left standing. Pierce was to explode them, of course. 'And if the Engineer's hoist with his own petard, Larry,' he said, ' 'tis into the seventh heaven I'll be blown, so you needn't fret.' God, to see that old fort go up! 'Twas as old as Cromwell, you know.

"Pierce used to be like a kid; he'd get dead earnest if anything went wrong, but up to three weeks before the end 'twas going as right as rain. 'The Gods are with us and all the saints!' he would say—he had sayings'd make you laugh. Then one night—the tenth of February, the Tans got him, coming from mother's house. They took him beyond Drumcondra and killed him—with bayonets—in a ditch.

"After that Ryan was in command. He was terrible good to me; he gave me all the work he could. I was no use for the digging because of my right arm—it was stiff since a bullet I got in May—but I used to bring in the guns.

"Exciting work it was, often enough, but I got on all right till the twenty-third. That night I was pulled off a tram by Auxiliaries and taken to Arbour Hill. I had nothing on me; all the same, being Pierce's brother I expected to be kept, but I was released next day.

"Well, of course, I didn't like the look of that—as if they'd got wind of something and I was to be watched. I thought 'twould break my heart to do it, but there was no way out; I sent word to Ryan and offered to give up the work.

"Ryan was kind—too kind, maybe, for such a job. Anyway he refused to cut me off. I daren't be kept in the city, but he'd send me to the hills, he said. He was afraid something had gone wrong; several of the outside staff had sent word they were being watched and daren't come to the house. There was only one thing to be done; he was sending to the

South for a gang of men who'd be unknown. It would put the whole business back a week; he fixed it for the sixth; the executions were to be on the eighth.

"The job he gave me was to meet the incoming men and direct them on. He gave me maps, timetables, countersigns and everything, arranged to send me despatches telling me when to expect the gangs and sent me to a safe little farmhouse in the hills.

"Well, I thought Pierce would have made a sounder plan; it seemed trusting too much to luck, having only one route, and if I was taken it would be bad, but 'twas a race against time now and everything had just to be done the quickest way.

"That last week five gangs came up and everything went like clockwork. A despatch would come from Ryan in the morning describing the men, where I was to meet them and so on, and each night, right enough, they came and I gave them the directions and sent them on.

"The best engineer we had was to come up from Cork to set and fire the mines. He was to come on Friday night—and at three o'clock on Saturday morning the attack would begin.

"Heartsick I was, you can imagine, not to be in at the end—not to help the fight or see the old gaol go up; but I knew I mustn't go in even with the last men, now I was known. Friday seemed a long day to me. To begin with, all morning, Ryan's despatch didn't come. By mid-day I got uneasy and went to see was there anyone on the road; I saw no one, the whole length of the Glen, and turned in again. There it was. A man had come with it, Mrs. Byrne said, the minute after I went out and he couldn't wait.

" 'Twas all in order, signed by Ryan. McKnight would arrive any time after dark—a tall, sandy man with a Scotch accent. He would bring credentials from the Southern Command; there would be two or three with him all disguised either as Auxiliaries or in khaki; they would travel in a British army lorry in order to get through the city after curfew, and appear to be raiding the house; they would be expected at the tunnel house by two o'clock; all the directions as to route, passwords and so on, I already knew; I was to wait for them at a place I had suggested myself, a waste house in the Glen called Murdoch's barn.

"I thought the day would never pass. I was too uneasy to make talk with the farm people and too uneasy to be alone. All the afternoon I went walking up and down the mountain, talking to Pierce in my mind. Any minute I could have cried. His great plan to be so near the end and he not to be there—all he was missing—all the triumph and joy. Maybe he would not miss it after all. I couldn't believe he was far away; there were times that day I'd have sworn I heard his voice—he was good to me ever and always. I felt a wonderful kindness and protection over me. At sunset I went down to the barn.

"It was a desolate, lonesome place, out of sight or sound of houses, in a hollow back off the road. The house had been burned down a year ago and only the barn and cowshed remained.

"The ladder up to the barn was broken. I mended it with a strong cord I had brought. Then I boarded up the windows and the cracks in the walls so that we could have lights, and mended the leg of the old bench, and made a table with two old barrels and a board. I stuck a candle on each end of my table; they'd be studying the maps; they didn't know, at all, till I would tell them, in what part of the city the tunnel was.

"I had a long wait then, and a dreary one while the shadows were closing on the Glen. There was nothing to interest you in the barn; the mice were shy, and I hated the thin squeak of the bats. The place had a cold, damp, earthy smell—you'd think you were in your grave.

" 'Twas partly the gloom of the place, I suppose, and partly the work being so nearly done; anyway the fit of horror and misery I'd been holding off since they murdered him fell on me there. The feeling he was living and watching and minding me was all gone—I could only think of his body, torn and horrible, in the grave—I felt alone and afraid—horribly afraid.

" 'Twas past eleven when I heard the lorry at last. I took my gun and stood at the top of the ladder for fear of genuine raiders instead of my men. I was satisfied though, when I saw the sandy head of the first man and heard the northern accent in his 'goodnight'.

"I lit the candles and looked at his credentials; two men followed him; they sat down. While they studied my maps I studied them.

"These men were taking the place of Pierce; there was a twist of jealousy, maybe, in my mind; or maybe 'twas the queer picture the three faces made, lit up by the flickering candle and nothing but black gloom behind; I took no liking to the men; I doubted were they big enough men for the job. McKnight had a clever face, sure enough, with sharp, close-set eyes, and he wore the Khaki as if to the manner born. The man on his left, whom he'd introduced as Brigadier Quinn, was a powerful looking fellow with black hair and a determined jaw—something the type of Mick. The third, Murphy, stared at me so hard that I couldn't well stare at him. He'd be called good-looking, I dare say—a smooth white face and dark eyes and a small black moustache.

"They were in a hurry, of course, to get done. McKnight questioned me in a quick, business-like way and kept saying 'Thanks, thanks,' as if glad to get my answers short and clear. Quinn was taking shorthand notes all the time. Murphy never took his eyes off me; he had a twitching muscle under the left eye that gave him an ugly look; it got on my nerves; I was bothered with a notion that I'd seen him before.

"McKnight folded the map and put it in his pocket—I'd not be wanting it again:

" 'You say the centre one is the tunnel house; is that where we knock?'

" 'No, no;' I answered, 'knock at the end house—number eighteen.'

" 'He told us that before,' Murphy said impatiently, and stood up. I noticed his arms then; they were too long. He was turning to go, but he glanced sharply at me and sat down again, whispering to McKnight.

"Then suddenly, the vague memory I'd had sharpened and stabbed into my brain. I had seen him, just so, whispering, in my mother's house, during a night raid; he was in khaki; Pierce had got out at the back, just in time—Pierce was there, standing behind him, in the shadow, leaning forward, his face white as death, pointing at him with his left hand—

" 'That is all?' McKnight asked, and I answered, 'That's all.'

"Then I remembered that Pierce was dead.

" 'What ails him?' Quinn whispered, looking at me.

"My heart had stopped. Then it beat and the thunder of it broke up my thoughts.

" 'Time to be off!' Murphy said in an urgent, angry tone, and he quenched the lights. The others said 'good-night'. They were at the door.

"Then, at last, I was able to use my brain; I turned and said, fairly steadily—'My God, I'd forgotten! A most important thing. Show me the map again!'

"McKnight came back impatiently. I lit a candle, fumbling, delaying, praying desperately. 'I'll mark them on the map,' I said, 'mines—our own mines—on Glencullen Road—'

"I heard Murphy give a low, chuckling laugh. 'Come with us,' he said, 'and point them out.'

"I wasn't thinking clearly—I thought that would do—to go with them, and, in some lonely place—it would be three

28

to one, but I could think of nothing else. I was going to say, 'That will do.' But I didn't say it; a hand gripped my arm—gentle and strong—Pierce's hand. I said then, 'I can't do that.'

"At that Murphy turned; he was the leader: 'No time to lose,' he said roughly: 'Bring him along!' He strode forward. I wheeled aside and got in the doorway and fired. I missed Murphy; Quinn fell.

"Murphy was on me then like a wild beast; his long arms were crushing me, like a baboon's; I'd have had small chance, even with two sound arms; he and McKnight got my gun.

"I had left cord hanging on the ladder; they tied me with it, feet and hands, and gagged me—I could hardly breathe—and flung me on my knees by the wall.

"I knelt up, struggling to free my hands. McKnight was leaning over Quinn. 'Curse you!' he muttered. 'He's dead!'

"Murphy turned on him with a snarl: 'You have yourself to blame! I told you the shortest way, why didn't you take it!'

"McKnight stood up. I could see his face by the light of the one candle, like Satan's, his teeth bared.

" 'By Hell,' he said, 'you can take it now!'

"I saw what was coming, clear and sure: myself lying dead there in the barn; those two on the road; a message to the Castle; those two at the house, knocking, giving the countersign, brought in. Then the fight—they'd let it begin—the prison surrounded—a massacre—howling devils slaughtering our men—the prisoners—I could see it all. And that would be Pierce's work—the end of his great plan—because they had trusted me and I was a fool.

"I don't know if I screamed; it was like the soul crying out in me as Murphy took aim—crying, 'Pierce! Pierce!'

" 'You're too damned like your brother,' he muttered; his face was black with hate. Then it twisted hideously and whitened and, his eyes rolled up and he shrieked—God, such a shriek. And never heard! And he flung himself, face down, on the floor, gasping and shuddering, in a fit.

"McKnight cried out, too, and dropped his gun and crouched in the far corner of the barn.

"The strength of two men came into me then. I got my hands free and my feet, tore the gag off and picked up a gun. I stood over McKnight; his teeth were chattering: 'Who was it?' he gasped.

"I answered, 'You know well who it was.'

"He began pleading for his life. Whoever had killed him it wasn't he—he had no hand in it—had tried to stop it— had done his best.

"I didn't believe him; I don't know why I didn't shoot him, but he was such a cowering, gibbering wretch. And I was tired. I stood covering him with my gun.

"Murphy was sprawled along the floor, quiet as a corpse.

"It wasn't long till the others came; they had been ambushed and lost a man. McKnight was there, a big, gentle, fellow, and O'Sullivan, the best friend Pierce had.

"They put the two prisoners in the lorry; Murphy was unconscious still. I was able to give them the directions, but not able to tell what had happened—I couldn't get it clear in my mind—I told them Pierce had come, forgetting that he was dead.

"I showed McKnight Ryan's despatch—it had been captured on the way to me and read, he supposed; he said it could do no more harm. They thought all should go right now. They had just time to get in.

"O'Sullivan made them leave me at the farm. I was tired, I can tell you! I slept well."

Mountjoy.

The Prisoner
(FOR E.C.)

It was on an evening late in May that Liam Daly startled us by strolling into Úna's room, a thin, laughing shadow of the boy we had known at home. We had imagined him a helpless convalescent still in Ireland and welcomed him as if he had risen from the dead. For a while there was nothing but clamourous question and answer, raillery, revelry and the telling of news; his thirty-eight days' hunger-strike had already become a theme of whimsical wit; but once or twice as he talked his face sobered and he hesitated, gazing at me with a pondering, burdened look.

"He holds me with his glittering eye!" I complained at last. He laughed.

"Actually," he said, "you're right. There is a story I have to tell—sometime, somewhere, and if you'll listen, I couldn't do better than to tell it here and now."

He had found an eager audience, but his grave face quieted us and it was in an intent silence that he told his inexplicable tale.

"You'll say it was a dream," he began, "and I hope you'll be right; I could never make up my mind; it happened in the gaol. You know Kilmainham?" He smiled at Larry who nodded. "The gloomiest prison in Ireland, I suppose—goodness knows how old. When the strike started I was in a punishment cell, a 'noisome dungeon', right enough, complete with rats and all, dark always, and dead quiet;

31

none of the others were in that wing. It amounted to solitary confinement, of course, and on hunger-strike that's bad, the trouble is to keep a hold of your mind.

"I think it was about the thirtieth day I began to be afraid—afraid of going queer. It's not a pretty story, all this," he broke off, looking remorsefully at Úna, "but I'd like you to understand—I want to know what you think.

"They'd given up bringing in food and the doctor didn't trouble himself overmuch with me; sometimes a warder would look through the peephole and shout a remark; but most of the day and all night I was alone.

"The worst was losing the sense of time; you've no idea how that torments you. I'd doze and wake up and not know whether a day or only an hour had gone; I'd think sometimes it was the fiftieth day, maybe, and we'd surely be out soon; then I'd think it was the thirtieth still; then a crazy notion would come that there was no such thing as time in prison at all; I don't know how to explain—I used to think that time went past outside like a stream, moving on, but in prison you were in a kind of whirlpool—time going round and round with you, so that you'd never come to anything, even death, only back again to yesterday and round to today and back to yesterday again. I got terrified, then, of going mad; I began talking and chattering to myself, trying to keep myself company, and that only made me worse because I found I couldn't stop—something seemed to have got into my brain and to be talking—talking hideous, blasphemous things, and I couldn't stop it. I thought I was turning into that—Ah, there's no describing it!

"At times I'd fight my way out of it and pray. I knew, at those times, that the blaspheming thing wasn't myself; I thought 'twas a foul spirit, some old criminal maybe, that had died in that cell. Then the fear would come on me that if I died insane he'd take possession of me and I'd get lost in Hell. I gave up praying for everything except the one thing, then—that I'd die before I went mad. One living soul to talk to would have saved me; when the doctor came I'd all I could do to keep from crying out to him not to leave me alone; but I'd just sense enough left to hold on while he was there.

"The solitude and the darkness were like one—the one enemy—you couldn't hear and you couldn't see. At times it was pitch black; I'd think I was in my coffin then and the silence trying to smother me. Then I'd seem to float up and away—to lose my body, and then wake up suddenly in a cold sweat, my heart drumming with the shock. The darkness and I were two things hating one another, striving to destroy one another—it closing on me, crushing me, stifling the life out of my brain—I trying to pierce it, trying to see—My God, it was awful!

"One black night the climax came. I thought I was dying and that 'twas a race between madness and death. I was striving to keep my mind clear till my heart would stop, praying to go sane to God. And the darkness was against me—the darkness, thick and powerful and black. I said to myself that if I could pierce that, if I could make myself see—see anything, I'd not go mad. I put out all the strength I had, striving to see the window or the peep-hole or the crucifix on the wall, and failed. I knew there was a little iron seat clamped into the wall in the corner opposite the bed. I willed, with a desperate, frenzied intensity, to see that; and I did see it at last. And when I saw it all the fear and strain died away in me, because I saw that I was not alone.

"He was sitting there quite still, a limp, despairing figure, his head bowed, his hands hanging between his knees; for a long time I waited, then I was able to see better and I saw that he was a boy—fair-haired, white-faced, quite young, and there were fetters on his feet. I can tell you, my heart went out to him, in pity and thankfulness and love.

"After a while he moved, lifted up his head and stared at me—the most piteous look I have ever seen.

"He was a young lad with thin, starved features and deep eye-sockets like a skull's; he looked, then bowed his head down hopelessly again, not saying a word. But I knew that his whole torment was the need to speak, to tell something; I got quite strong and calm, watching him, waiting for him to speak.

"I waited a long while, and that dizzy sense of time working in a circle took me, the circles getting larger and larger, like eddies in a pool, again. At last he looked up and rested his eyes beseechingly on me as if imploring me to be patient; I understood; I had conquered the dark—he had to break through the silence—I knew it was very hard.

"I saw his lips move and at last I heard him—a thin, weak whisper came to me: 'Listen—listen—for the love of God!'

"I looked at him, waiting; I didn't speak; it would have scared him. He leaned forward, swaying, his eyes wed, not on mine, but on some awful vision of their own; the eyes of a soul in purgatory, glazed with pain.

" 'Listen, listen!' I heard, 'the truth! You must tell it—it must be remembered; it must be written down!'

" 'I will tell it,' I said, very gently, 'I will tell it if I live.'

" 'Live, live, and tell it!' he said, moaningly and then, then he began. I can't repeat his words, all broken, shuddering phrases; he talked as if to himself only—I'll remember as best I can.

" 'My mother, my mother!' he kept moaning, and 'the name of shame!' 'They'll put the name of shame on us,' he said, 'and my mother that is so proud—so proud she never let a tear fall, though they murdered my father before her eyes! Listen to me!' He seemed in an anguish of haste and fear, striving to tell me before we'd be lost again. 'Listen! Would I do it to save my life? God knows I wouldn't, and I won't! But they'll say I did it! They'll say it to her. They'll be pouring out their lies through Ireland and I cold in my grave!'

"His thin body was shaken with anguish; I didn't know what to do for him. At last I said, 'Sure, no one'll believe their lies.'

" 'My Lord won't believe it!' he said vehemently. 'Didn't he send me up and down with messages to his lady? Would he do that if he didn't know I loved him—know I could go to any death?'

" ' 'Twas in the Duke's Lawn they caught me,' he went on. ' 'Twas on Sunday last and they're starving me ever since; trying night and day they are to make me tell them what house he's in—and God knows I could tell them! I could tell!'

"I knew well the dread that was on him. I said, 'There's no fear,' and he looked at me a little quieter then.

" 'They beat me,' he went on. 'They half strangled me in the Castle Yard and then they threw me in here. Listen to me! Are you listening?' he kept imploring. 'I'll not have time to tell you all!'

" 'Yesterday one of the red-coats came to me—an officer, I suppose, and he told me my Lord will be caught. Some lad that took his last message sold him . . . He's going to Moira House in the morning, disguised; they'll waylay him—attack him in the street. They say there'll be a fight—and sure I know there will—and he'll be alone; they'll kill him. He laughed, the devil—telling me that! He laughed, I tell you, because I cried.

" 'A priest came in to me then—a priest! My God, he was a fiend! He came into me in the dead of night, when I was lying shivering and sobbing for my Lord. He sat and talked to me in a soft voice—I thought at first he was kind.

Listen till I tell you! Listen till you hear all! He told me I could save my Lord's life. They'd go quietly to his house and take him; there'd be no fighting and he'd not be hurt. I'd only have to say where his lodging was. My God, I stood up and cursed him! He, a priest! God forgive me if he was.'

" 'He was no priest,' I said, trying to quiet him. 'That's an old tale.'

" 'He went out then,' the poor boy went on, talking feverishly, against time. 'And a man I'd seen at the Castle came in, a man with a narrow face and a black cloak. The priest was with him and he began talking to me again, the other listening, but I didn't mind him or answer him at all. He asked me wasn't my mother a poor widow, and wasn't I her only son. Wouldn't I do well to take her to America, he said, out of the hurt and harm, and make a warm home for her, where she could end her days in peace. I could earn the right to it, he said—good money, and the passage out, and wasn't it my duty as a son. The face of my mother came before me—the proud, sweet look she has, like a queen; I minded the loving voice of her and she saying, "I gave your father for Ireland and I'd give you." My God, my God, what were they but fiends? What will I do, what will I do at all?'

"He was in an agony, twisting his thin hands.

" 'You'll die and leave her her pride in you,' I said.

"Then, in broken gasps he told me the rest. 'The Castle man—he was tall, he stood over me—he said, "You'll tell us what we want to know."

" 'I'll die first,' I said to him and he smiled. He had thin, twisted lips—and he said, "You'll hang in the morning like a dog."

" 'Like an Irishman, please God,' I said.

"He went mad at that and shook his fist in my face and talked sharp and wicked through his teeth. O my God! I went down on my knees to him, I asked him in God's holy name! How will I bear it? How will I bear it at all?

"He was overwhelmed with woe and terror; he bowed his head and trembled from head to foot.

" 'They'll hang me in the morning,' he gasped, looking at me haggardly. 'And they'll take him and they'll tell him I informed. The black priest'll go to my mother—he said it! Himself said it! He'll tell her I informed! It will be the death blow on her heart—worse than death! 'Twill be written in the books of Ireland to the end of time. They'll cast the word of shame on my grave.'

"I never saw a creature in such pain—it would break your heart. I put out all the strength I had and swore an oath to him. I swore that if I lived I'd give out the truth, get it told and written through Ireland. I don't know if he heard; he looked at me wearily, exhausted, and sighed and leaned his head back against the wall.

"I was tired out and half-conscious only, but there was a thing I was wanting to ask. For a while I couldn't remember what it was, then I remembered again and asked it: 'Tell me, what is your name?'

"I could hardly see him. The darkness had taken him again, and the silence; his voice was very far off and faint.

" 'I forget,' it said. 'I have forgotten. I can't remember my name.'

"It was quite dark then. I believe I fainted. I was unconscious when I was released."

Max Barry broke the puzzled silence with a wondering exclamation: "Lord Edward! More than a hundred years!"

"Poor wretch!" laughed the irrepressible Frank. "In Kilmainham since ninety-eight!"

"Ninety-eight?" Larry looked up quickly. "You weren't in the hospital were you, Liam? I was. You know it used to be the condemned cell. There's a name carved on the window-sill, and a date in ninety-eight—I can't—I can't remember the name."

"Was there anyone accused, Max?" Úna asked.

"Any record of a boy?"

Max frowned: "Not that I remember—but so many were suspect—it's likely enough—poor boy!"

"I never could find out," said Liam. "Of course I wasn't far off delirium. It may have been hallucination or a dream."

I did not believe he believed that and looked at him. He smiled.

"I want you to write it for me," he pleaded quietly. "I promised, you see."

Mountjoy and Kilmainham.

The Return of Niav
(FOR L.S.)

An air from Errigal seemed to come to America with Maeve; that beauty of hers that subdued the heart like dé Danaan magic had changed with the sorrowful years; like sunrise once, she had a more troubled, patient, tender loveliness now. "Like to the mournful moon," Úna said.

The evenings she spent with us were wonderful, all the world's wars forgotten in the talk we had always loved—talk of the enchanted waters and hills of Ireland, of ruins and symbols and rituals and of the music that would come out of Ireland when we were free.

"Do you know that my Neoineen is making the strangest, most marvellous music already?" she said. "Her masters in Leipzig hardly know what to make of her; she is as creative, they told me, at seventeen as any composer in his prime, and makes deliriously beautiful tunes. But she won't study; while she should have been learning the history of music she was composing a symphony, I'm afraid!"

"What is her symphony?" Úna asked, and Maeve replied: "The Children of Lir."

She looked at us then, her eyes shining, and spoke in a voice hushed with joy. "It is the sweetest, unearthliest music I have ever heard. The cold—the mortal cold of the waters! The wild lonely sorrow of the swans—the yearning for human things—the dreadful enchanted striving through water and air—nothing could describe it but music—no music but hers! She will be giving the music of Ireland to the world."

Maeve stopped, shy of so praising her own child, but I could believe it all. I had a memory of Neoineen when she was four years old and the loveliest thing, except her mother, that I had ever seen—a wind-sprite of a child with a floss of silvery-gold hair raying out like Lugh's halo round her head, and a little pointed face and dark hazel eyes. Her soul and body were all music; day-long she would be dancing to the sun or the wind or the moon, or making strange little rhymes. Maeve was making a little pagan of her, filling her imagination with the wonder-tales of Ireland, inventing druid rituals, making magical songs. I remembered an old priest warning Maeve solemnly that she was exposing her child to influences more dangerous than she knew and how Maeve, who always had an artist's recklessness, only laughed—"All beautiful things are good."

"Do you remember," I asked her, "how anxious you used to make poor Father Cahill? He thought Neoineen would lose her soul!"

I spoke laughingly, but Maeve's face, remembering, grew grave. "You don't know," she said, "how nearly he was right."

She looked at our incredulous faces and smiled, "You don't believe it? I will tell you then—I will tell you, though I was dreadfully to blame, because it is all over long ago. I think that was how her music came."

We drew close, intent, waiting, and dreamily she began to tell.

"It never could have happened but for the solitude of our home: I was so eager to welcome a companion for Neoineen. I built my house there for the glorious freedom of the place—a place unchanged, you would think, since the days of Fionn. Our home is on the very brow of the mountain where it breaks in a cliff over the loch—the water at our feet, the hawks and the clouds and the mountain peaks overhead, and steep, wooded ravines and torrents below. There we lived, just our two selves and my old Maura, as happy as human people could ever be. We had no neighbours at all except half-a-dozen families who lived fighting the mountain for a livelihood on their tiny farms. A little scamp called Seumas belonging to one of them was Neoineen's only playmate. I liked him to come because he talked such delicious Irish—I did not want her to hear English at all—but she preferred playing with me or alone.

"It was unthinkable, always, to leave Neoineen to the companionship of a nurse, impossible to find a satisfying playmate for such a child.

"That summer—the thing happened when she was five—we had the most radiant June I have ever known, full of wild scents of heather and bog, and we spent golden days. I was painting trees at the edge of the Druid's Wood—a steep, narrow glen—and Neoineen used to wander away by herself on marvellous adventures.

"We were in the Fionn cycle then! She was Osgar, I think, and I was Oisín; I was expected to make a new song every day!

"St. John's Eve came, one of our Festivals; a morning of jewel colours in earth and sky. We had planned to stay out till moonrise and light our magical fire in the ravine and we had made a song with a sweet, bewitching little tune to it, to lure the fairies to our fire. While I settled to my painting Neoineen wandered away to gather wood of nine different kinds and to choose a place for the fire. She was a long time away, but she came to my whistle at last, wearing a foxglove helmet on every finger, and with her arms full of wet flowers—meadow-sweet and the yellow irises that grow in pools.

" 'How did you pull those, Osgar?' I asked, and she answered:

" 'Niav brought them from Tír-na-n-Óg. I found Niav in the wood; she sang a most wondrous song.'

"I was accustomed to Neoineen's 'wondrous' adventures and only thought, while she told me her tale, eating her lunch under a tree, that it was the prettiest she had invented yet. She was impatient to be away, and jumped up very soon. 'Farewell, Fionn!' she called to me, kissing her hand as she ran away into the wood, and, guessing that our roles had changed, I answered, 'Farewell, Oisín!'

"You know what the silence of noon can be, the spell-bound silence of a June day; it seems to well up, like clear water, from earth to heaven and hold one entranced under a still pool—it is in those silences great music is born.

"It was such a magical silence that was pierced then, suddenly, by the most rapturous music I had ever heard, wild singing, joyous and daring as a bird's. As I listened; scarcely breathing, fantastic images thronged my mind; I thought some wild swan must be singing his death-song, having strayed out of Tír-na-n-Óg. I thought it was faery music out of the mountain—I thought of Étaín and of Niav . . .

"The singer was coming towards me through the wood; Neoineen was holding her by the hand; I could see her between the trees. Her beauty was like the beauty of her song—daring and exquisite and free. A little high head she had with a glory of red-gold hair about it; a green, ragged gown was on her and her delicate white feet and arms were bare; she came towards me like some young, triumphant queen, leading her lover by the hand; she looked at me with soft eyes like a fawn's and smiled.

"Come with us to Tír-na-n-Óg," Neoineen said, and took my hand and led me down the steep, dark paths into the wood. 'This is Niav,' she said, speaking Irish, of course, and the girl looked at me joyously and said, '*Cuirim fad beannacht na gréine thú!*'—'I give you the blessing of the sun!' Her Irish was as musical as her song, soft and vigorous and rich.

"She led us down to a deep hollow in the wood, honey-fragrant, alight with the smouldering purple of foxglove, loud with the babble of a little waterfall where the brook tumbled into a pool. There, on a great flat stone, they had prepared the druid fire.

"The foxgloves were Oisín's warriors, it seemed; he went from one to another, praising them for marvellous deeds, bidding Niav lean down and kiss the best; I heard her add her praise to Oisín's with such queenly grace, speak so gravely of their perils and wounds that I became almost rapt in their illusion, too. When it was over she came and sat in a patch of pure sunlight, singing dreamy and mystical songs—songs such as I had never heard before, though I knew Irish music well—more entrancing than any I had heard.

"I spoke to her once, 'You have Irish only?' I said, and 'Irish only,' she replied.

"Tired of singing, she ran to Neoineen and they chased one another like sungleams among the trees. Neoineen like a little mad sprite of laughter, growing wilder and wilder, till she tumbled, poor baby, into the pool. Niav gave a strange, terrified cry, but Neoineen scrambled out, laughing, and shook herself like a dog. I hurried her home, leaving Niav among the trees.

"It had been an enchanted day, but it ended sadly. Neoineen had set her heart on the druid fire—she was a fire-worshipper always; but the evening was chilly and she seemed fevered with excitement and I dared not, after that wetting, let her stay out after dark. She tried all ways to persuade me, but at last, to Fionn's sorrow, Oisín cried. I remember the play I made to comfort her, with the song we had made to sing in the druid wood. She was a faery

43

child and I was a lonely woman with no little girl and when I sang our luring little song she would creep out of faeryland, steal to me and leap into my arms at last. Again and again we played it until, drowsy and serene again, she let me sing her to sleep.

"I hardly know how to tell you how the rest of that summer passed; it is like a half-forgotten dream. Only I know that for me no less than for Neoineen there was a childish eagerness in living, a joyous wonder, from day to day—as though we lived to music. 'Niav'—we knew no other name for her, played with Neoineen and sang for me, sat in the sunlight or crouched over my fire, telling long tales, as though they were dear memories, of the old glories of the Gael. It was all what my heart's desire for Neoineen would have chosen. I listened and watched their play and painted and forgot there were sorrows in the world.

"Then, in September, quite suddenly, my dear old godmother died. She brought us up, you know—me and Hugo Blake; he was left desolate by her death. He wrote and implored me to go to him; he had always regarded me as his elder sister and he had no one else in the world. I had to go; and I had to leave Neoineen.

"I know you will think I was to blame; I know it myself now. I could have taken her, of course; but Hugo was in one of his dark, gloomy moods, and his Tower seemed no place for a child, and she was so happy, playing with Niav.

"Niav's own folk, she had told us, lived 'over the hill'. Quite poor, I imagined them, since she wore thin, ragged clothes always and could not read or write; but the gentlest, in the West, are the very poor, and Niav was as gentle as a queen. I left Neoineen to her and Maura, and went to Hugo for two months.

"He was ill and despairing. It was one of those black periods when he could not paint; there were times, you know, when we feared for his mind. November was over before I came home.

"It was a troubled letter from Maura that brought me then.

" 'The darling is as good as gold,' she wrote, 'but she's not taking her food and she's too thin. She does be falling asleep in the middle of her play.'

"To my disappointment she was asleep when I came home, lying on a nest of cushions by the fire, Niav on guard. Niav rose and kissed me softly. At the very sight of her shining, serene loveliness, the old gladness flowed back, and when my Neoineen awoke and hugged me and caressed me, crooning little lyrics of her love, earth was my heaven again.

"But she was not well, my little one. I accused myself for staying so long away. Loving and contented as ever, she seemed, but she had not grown a hair's breadth and had lost weight and had become fastidious about food. Niav lived on with us; I could not do without her; no one else could make Neoineen eat at all. She never tired of the child; they would play together just as vividly, run just as lightly over the frosty ground as in those golden summer days; but after their play Neoineen would steal in to me tired—even, I sometimes fancied, a little nervous, and cuddle into my arms and fall asleep. She slept at night too deeply; nothing would wake her; her breathing was too light.

"My old friend, Dr. Moore, came for a day or two, but he could not give me much help. The child's imagination seemed over-excited, he said, he found nothing else wrong.

"It was then that I began to wonder about Niav, to watch her closely and love her not quite so well—she seemed to me to have changed. She who had been so tender would not comprehend that Neoineen was ill, would not listen to my fears.

"I began to be afraid of their play, though it had grown so dreamy and quiet you would have thought it could not hurt Neoineen. One day I came upon them suddenly in the shrubbery, Neoineen lying on a bed of fallen leaves. Her eyes were shut, her arms lay limp, her face was quite colour-less. I was frightened; I could not wake her or make her stir. Niav laughed at me, a little scornfully I thought. 'She is only playing! Come back, Asthore!' At that soft whisper in Niav's sweetest tones, Neoineen awoke and clung to me and cried. I looked at Niav then for the first time, coldly, and said, 'Do not play at death with her again!' She did not answer save with a smiling look, but to my imagination there was a mocking challenge in her eyes.

"My own imagination was growing morbid—tainted with jealousy perhaps—that is what I thought then. It was foolish; my Neoineen loved me; she loved no one so well as me; yet if Niav left her, I believed, so entwined was she with her life, the child would die. Then again I thought myself half-crazy in that belief, so unreasoning, so fantastical it seemed. And as the dread took hold of me, haunted me more and more terribly—the dread that I was doomed to lose Neoineen, it was my own feverish imagina-tion that I accused. 'The more need for her,' I would say to myself then, 'to have a clear-spirited, joyous being like Niav to share her play.' So, in a nightmare duel between warning instinct and incredulous will, I wore the winter and spring away.

"Of all festivals of the year, except Saint John's Eve, we loved Beltaine best. It was then, on the last day of April, that the crisis came.

"All the Beltaine mysteries—the fire-building and songs and rituals, Neoineen had decided, were to be a surprise for me. She and Niav would prepare them alone. So all that day they were away together in the Druid Wood. They were away so long that I went out at dusk to look for them, calling 'Neoineen, Neoineen!'

"Do you remember April evenings in that glen? The sky translucent like a green faery sea, the mountain like a rock of amethyst, cut into hollow and ridge, shadow and gleam—and that evening there was a ghost of new moon. Green the woods were, too, just sprinkled with budding leaves, seeming to hold the dying light in a magical net; the long weeds and brambles were cold with dew and a silvery mist was winding among the trees. There was something tremulous, eager, pent, in the listening air.

"I stole down, calling softly, into the deep glen, till I heard the gurgle of water among the stones and came out where the little torrent breaks into a fall—where we made our Saint John's fire on the Druid stone.

"There on the flat stone lay Neoineen, in her thin white smock, quite still. Kneeling upright beside her, her hands clasped, swaying and singing softly, was Niav; my heart stood still.

"For a moment such terror was on me that I could only stand motionless, watching, while Niav laid her kiss on the child's mouth. Then I rushed down, screaming, and seized Neoineen and cried out I know not what fierce things to the girl, telling her to go back to where she came from, that never, never, should she touch or see my darling again. Niav stood up then and lifted her head and laughed—a low sweet laughter—and turned and ran and vanished into the dark.

"For dreadful hours Maura and I worked, wrapping her in hot blankets, chafing her numbed body and stiffened limbs, forcing warm milk between her clenched teeth, before the rigor passed. Her little face was terrible; I could scarcely look at it; blue and shrunken it was, like an old woman's—like a cunning old woman, dead.

"When we had won our battle with death—when her breathing was tranquil at last, and her blood flowing, and

47

her body warm and relaxed in natural sleep, I stole into bed and held her fast in my arms. Life is wonderful when you have looked at death.

"It was late in the morning when I opened the curtains; sunlight flowed over her as she lay, and gleamed on her shining hair. As I stood, looking down at her, crying with love and joy, she opened her eyes and looked right into mine. I had been through terror, but that moment was the most horrible I have known. What looked at me out of those hazel eyes was mockery—it was mockery—triumphant—and hate.

"I turned away to the window, gasping, pressing my forehead to the cool pane, praying that I might not be mad—I tried to force myself to call her and dress her and brush her hair, chatting merrily as every day; but I could not. I knelt and held her by the shoulders at last and looked into her face and said sharply, 'Neoineen, tell me what is wrong!' She smiled. 'Nothing, Mameen,' she said softly, 'nothing, little Queen-Mother, nothing at all!' It was her lovingest name for me; it froze me to hear it spoken in that bitter-sweet tone. I tried to startle her—to shake the strange mood away; I said suddenly, 'Do you know Niav is gone?'

" 'Niav has gone away,' she answered lightly.

" 'We don't want Niav any more.' And she fixed me with those cold, hard eyes till my heart shrank.

"Little Seumas was calling from the garden, wild with eagerness over the May-day games. But there was no festival of Beltaine; she laughed and called and chased him up and down hill, hid and sprang out at him from trees and boulders, hooting like an owl, crying out like a curlew until he was bewildered and tired. She caught him then and laughed, but he turned and stared at her and pulled himself free and stole away home, afraid. I told her she had been rough and unkind, and she cried.

"I blamed myself bitterly then. I should have been thankful I said; it was just that her long illness had suddenly gone. Day by day now she grew healthier, browner; she ate, greedily even—was never tired—never for one moment fretted for Niav, never even mentioned her name. I walked and played, explored and gardened, sang and danced with her as of old; she went with me everywhere, responsive, caressing as ever before—yet—yet—Oh, how can I tell you the truth of those hideous days? I did not believe in her, did not want her, did not love her. I was consumed and tortured with craving for my own little lovely girl.

"I dare say I am not remembering it all quite as it was. I am sure, whatever other thing had happened, my own mind was unbalanced, my imagination distorted from the strain.

"Maura told me that I should bring Niav back. 'What she done,' Maura said, 'no other can undo,' and I used to walk wildly about the mountain seeking and enquiring for any sign, but the cottage folk knew nothing of her at all. One old woman drew from me the whole dreadful story; she sat in her corner distressfully shaking her head. 'You were mad foolish, mad foolish,' she said, 'you to lead her by the hand into your home.'

" 'What can I do?' I sobbed, 'what can I do to get my baby again?'

" 'I heard of them going,' she answered mournfully, 'but I never heard of one coming back.'

"I began, after crazy weeks of vain searching, to despair and try to comfort myself in childish ways, talking to Neoineen when I was quite alone, pretending that I held her in my arms. And I used to dream about her all night long—cruel, maddening dreams. I would hear her crying out to me, see her, reaching piteous arms to me from the dark, and always when I clasped her she turned to air.

"A kind of mania seized me to be going to the places where we had been together, repeating the things we had done; and the child followed me everywhere—the child that I hated—hated, now.

"I gathered wood of nine kinds on Saint John's Eve and set a fire in the glade on the druid's stone.

"Memory was vivid as an illusion—I thought there was music in the air. It was a day as golden as a year ago it had been, the air sweet with honeysuckle and with the songs of the water and the birds; there were foxgloves burning in the shadows, meadowsweet and irises in the pools. All the afternoon I was pulling weeds and flowers, strewing them around the druid stone, and sobbing, sobbing aloud. The child followed me, staring, scared and subdued; I tried to send her away, but she would not go. At moonrise I lit the fire and cried out the wild little invocation that Neoineen and I had made—gave way to all the crazy anguish within me—chanted it loud enough for the hills to hear. I was the forlorn mother in our story, playing alone, alone.

"The little brown girl sat crouching under a stone, whimpering with fear and cold. I cared nothing for her. I wanted my own baby, the child of my body and soul, wanted her more than the dying could long for life or the living for death, wanted her with an anguish that is not known.

"I flung my arms out in the darkness, walking nine times, sun-wise around the fire, singing, singing that luring, magical song; piercing sweet was the wild tune we had made!

"In the dark ravine the sparks leaped redly, terrifying the crouching child. As I passed her she sprang up shrieking and stamped her feet, but I sang on and flung ashes over her out of the fire. With a weird scream she fled from me into the darkness and I ended my ninth circling of the stone.

"When I stood still at last all was silent, and, suddenly frightened, I ran down to the stream. She was lying under the water with shut eyes.

"I lifted her; she was limp, white, unconscious. I carried her to the fire, stripped and warmed her, held her in the glow, wrapped her in my shawl, then carried her home, hugged to my heart, calling her every name she had ever heard—my star-flower, my daisy-bud, vein of my heart. Just as I crossed the threshold she opened her eyes, wide and loving and clear, but they filled with tears and she clung to me crying: 'Mameen, Mameen! Oh, hold me, little Queen-Mother! Don't let me go any more.' Then she fell asleep in my arms—my baby girl.

"No memory remains of it at all; it is gone like a dream."

Kilmainham.

De Profundis
(FOR L. O'B.)

"Some evening," Father Martin had promised us, "I will tell you a story as strange, though not, maybe, as adventurous, as any you have been telling here. I'll tell you how it was I began studying for the priesthood—I that was a self-willed, rebellious boy."

It was hard to imagine Father Martin as the rough boy he described; we had never known him save as a priest consumed with the ardour of his mission, an impassioned herald of eternity whom the sight of the world's worldliness made desperate. "I do not want to win!" he actually broke out, one night to Liam. "Ireland struggling, praying, suffering persecution, is holy—Ireland victorious might become this!" And he looked down on the busy Philadelphian thoroughfare with despair. None of us, of course, shared his fear, but we called him "fanatic" and forgave his malediction. We knew that Ireland had his potent prayers.

He told us his story one night in June; we understood better after hearing it, his sense of the unreality of all but immortal things.

"I wonder do you know at all," he began, "the sort of starved, ragged little farmhouse that was our home? My father died when we were all small—nine of us; God knows how my mother reared and fed us, and I never knew the light of kindness to leave her eyes.

52

"I was seventeen when the sickness came, following a season of half famine. It was one of those epidemics that doctors call influenza; our people used to call it the 'Black Death'; it swooped on Killerane as fatally that spring as it fell everywhere, later, during the war. The old people didn't seem to take it; 'twas the young that died. My sister Rosie was eighteen—the eldest of us; she came home with it from nursing a neighbour and in three days she died.

"I think the fear that gripped me then was worse than the grief; though I'd not been a good son to her, my mother was my queen of the world; when the thought came to me that she'd take it I would shake from head to foot. And two days after Rosie's funeral she took to her bed.

"The children were lost altogether; Nora, the next to myself, was fourteen; there wasn't a soul anywhere to help. The doctor looked in twice; he was going like a wild rider over the whole town-land and had dead or dying in nearly every house. He said then 'twould be no use coming again. The Priest gave her the last Sacraments on Sunday; he was sorry for us, but he could do no more; he had two parishes on his hands.

"All day I sat by her and watched her gasping away her life, watched the wildness of fever in her eyes, breaking my heart with dread and longing for the wise, happy mother I knew. There were children crying in every corner of the house, and poor little Nora, stealing out and in, like a lost soul.

"I had neither faith nor hope in me that night. I went outside; I remember the sweet, soft wind from the bogs, and the brave wide sky, all flying clouds, taking their share of gold and silver from the moon, and I remember that instead of praising God I had anger and blasphemy in my heart.

"I was not content to lose my mother; I was not content for her to go to Heaven. 'What'll Heaven be to her,'

I was raging, 'and her children trailing the cold roads of the world?'

"God forgive me, I was full always of heretical thoughts; 'twas a heart-break to my mother, and well I knew it, that I was not fit to be a priest. 'And if I had the vocation, have you the money?' I used to say to her roughly, and she would answer patiently: 'If you had the will, Avic, God would send the way.' But for all that, I always loved serving Mass. I was thinking over it, miserable, out there in the wind, swearing that if she'd get well I'd be good.

"Little Bridie came creeping and told me to go in. I went in to my mother in the little room; she was lying white, exhausted, her hands clutching the coverlet, and she looked up at me with an awful, despairing look in her eyes. The tears were streaming down my face. She got out some words at last:

" 'Did you ask Father Doherty to say Mass?'

"Well I had not asked him any such thing, because there were three shillings only in the house and, in the black mood I was in, I thought it might be better spent.

"Mother moaned when I shook my head. 'Nothing else'll save me,' she said. 'If he'd say a Mass before morning—I'd maybe get well.'

"Nora pulled me by the sleeve and whispered, 'You should go for the Priest.'

"I thought there was no sense in it at all.

" 'Is it walk the six miles,' I said, 'to Killerane? And I'd not get him at the house then; night and day he is visiting round. And I'll not leave her to die on me, and I away.'

"But mother looked up at me again, so piteous, it would break your heart, and moaned, 'O Martin, son, if you ever loved me, get the Priest to say Mass.'

"Well, I gave her a kiss—choked with sobbing I was, and left her. I thought I'd not see her alive again.

"I'll not forget that dark walk to Killerane, struggling up the long, steep hills, the wind wrestling with me every step; half cursing, I was and half praying, crying out loud, like a child.

"It was midnight when I got to Killerane and the Priest's house was dark. When the woman opened the door at last she was as cross as a bag of cats. 'He's away to Carrigroe,' she snapped, 'and he'll be going on to O'Flaherty's after that—didn't he give your mother the Sacraments the day and what more does she want? Go after him now if you wish,' said she, 'but it'll be time lost.'

" 'Tell him,' I said to her, 'that I came asking a Mass, and there's three shillings and I'll work out the rest.'

" 'I'll tell him,' said she, 'but he should have his Masses promised for a week at least, with four dead and nine dying,' and she shut the door.

"I didn't know what to do. I knew 'twould be useless going to Carrigroe—he'd have the Masses promised right enough. But to go back to my mother and tell her I could get no Mass—that I couldn't face. And if I went to O'Flaherty's, five miles on, when I'd go back she'd be dead.

"I stood at the gate in the dark road, praying—'God help me, what'll I do?' Then I started for Carrigroe.

"Sour thoughts I had in my heart; 'twas as if a devil had got into me, filling me with wrath and hate.

" 'Why couldn't Mrs. O'Flaherty die and be let die?' I was saying—'A bitter woman that would put blackness between you and the sun, not my mother that has the warmth and kindness of the sun itself!'

"Going from the Priest's house to Carrigroe I had to go past the graveyard and the chapel that stood away from the road in a dark grove of old trees. I was not a nervous boy; many's the time I had mocked the whispers of my school-fellows about that old graveyard and challenged them to pass through it at night; but the thought of my sister Rosie—she that had been singing at her work a week ago, shut down under the black mould, suddenly clutched me with horror, and when I thought of a grave to be dug for mother—couldn't stand it—I began to run.

"Did you ever experience panic—the real, primeval terror which the Greeks meant by the word? All nature seems to be chasing you, overtaking you with some awful, malignant purpose; you fly from it, but every bush and stone you leave behind rises to follow and destroy you—at last you fall. I fell to the ground just at the chapel gate.

"There my senses came to me again; I lay resting, wondering, with peace and comfort flowing into my soul. The narrow chapel windows were all lighted; streaming out against the tall trees it was—a soft, clear, yellow light.

"It never crossed my mind how strange it was, the candles to be lighting at that hour; I walked as quietly as I could up the avenue and went in through the open door. I knelt down in the last pew. The chapel was silent; there was not a soul in it but myself; but the altar candles were all lighted and the light of them seemed to shine in on my heart. I was full of peace and faith and I prayed.

"I knew I had to wait a little while. The wine was ready on the little table; at last, from the Sacristy, unattended, came the priest.

"It was a priest I had never seen before, much taller than Father Doherty, very old, with a high forehead and long white hair. He moved slowly; he came down to the altar-rails and stood looking mournfully down the aisle; I thought he looked terribly sad and worn. I rose up and came to him and when he saw me a great look of joy and wonder came into his face. I went up and took my place, kneeling at the altar-rails.

" 'My mother,' I said, looking up at him, and he bowed his head and I knew that he understood. Then the Mass began.

"I was a bit drowsy, I suppose, and my mind was full of my own trouble; I went through the first part of my service like a dream. But the strange voice of the priest caught me out of it—the deep aching tones, like the voice of a lost soul. I never heard Mass said as he was saying it, before or since—like one crying out for mercy, alone with God. His fervour gave me power, too, and I prayed as had never prayed, for all sinners, and for him: '*Misereatur tui omnipotens Deus, et dimissis peccatis tuis, perdurat te ad vitam aeternam.*' I prayed it with all my strength, and with a deep, awful sigh he said, 'Amen.'

"But after the Offertory the trouble went; his face changed; it became luminous with a kind of holy peace and a wonderful music came into his voice; he said, '*Ite missa est,*' with a slow, wondering joy, then, '*Deo gratias*'— a cry of thanksgiving; and at the end he chanted the 'De Profundis' like a triumphant song.

"I grew faint and blind under the power and strangeness of him; when all was over I went down and knelt at the altar-rails with my head down on my arms; I was trembling under a revelation—a light from another world.

"I felt that he was near, leaning over me, but I dared not look up at him; I heard him speak.

" 'My son,' he said, in a voice full of joy and love, 'you have released me from my long penance at last. Night after night for uncounted decades I have waited and found no server to serve this Mass. Remember when your time comes to celebrate this Mystery, a poor soul who for one promise broken, one Mass forgotten, was exiled for unnumbered years from God. Pray for me; I have prayed for you.'

"He left me; there was a long quietness and I prayed. When I looked up at last the Chapel was in darkness and very cold. I was shivering. I went to the door in a great hurry to get home, but it was locked; there was no way out.

"I suppose I fell asleep there on the floor. The caretaker woke me in the morning, sprinkling holy water on my face. 'Twas a grand, sunny, airy day and I ran the whole way home.

"Mother was lying awake, quite easy, and she gave me the loveliest smile when I went in. I told her nothing, then, but that a Mass had been said for her. I told her all the day I was ordained."

By God's Mercy
(FOR A.M.)

Maeve had brought with her from Ireland, in the capacity of maid, a girl from the wilderness of Clare. I saw her one day at Maeve's hotel and could not afterwards forget the sweet, sallow little face and great suffering eyes; I had never seen, in a young face, such resignation mingled with such pain. Her name, Maeve told me, was Nannie Maher. "A dear, splendid girl," she said. "We talk and lecture and write, but it is people like Nannie who are winning Ireland's war." She brought her to the studio one Sunday night.

At first Nannie was a little shy, but very soon with talk of folk and places that they both knew, Úna and she made friends; her shyness gave way to a soft garrulity and she began to talk about her brother, Brian, and "the boys".

"I would like you to tell my friends about Brian," Maeve said to her then: "I think it should be remembered; I think it should all be written down—would you mind?"

"I'd like well," Nannie answered simply, and with the frank, gracious candour of the West, she began telling us one of those tragic little stories of Ireland's war that are forgotten only because so many are told.

" 'Twas four months ago it happened," she said. "That time my mother and I were mostly alone. A hard winter it was for us, too, for we'd no near neighbours and Brian was away."

"With a flying column?" Frank asked, and Nannie answered, "He was with the Chief. The murder-gang were after the Chief that time and they'd got word he was in the West; the boys were terrible anxious and careful of him; Brian knew the country well and, young and all as he was, they'd appointed him guard. My poor mother didn't know where he was or when she'd see him at all, and there were times she would sit by the fire crying to herself for the loneliness and the dread. The best times would be when the lads from the column would come to us for a night's rest; a good rest we were able to give them too, for we were never raided, God be praised; the military took no notice of us at all.

"Well that day, early in the morning, when I was wetting the tea for breakfast, didn't Brian walk in. I near dropped the pot with the wonder and delight and when mother came in with eggs didn't she drop them in earnest to see him standing there laughing on the floor! Grand he was looking too—a proud, shining look on him, the way I knew he had great news.

" 'Guess who is coming to you the night?' says he, and I said, joking him, 'From the importance of the air you have it should be the Chief!' 'And the Chief it is,' says he.

"He sat down to his breakfast then and told us about it. I'll never forget the meal he ate! The poor lad was ravenous; 'twas a week since he got a meal under a roof. He told us the Chief was ill—not too bad, but needing a couple of days' rest and a quiet place where he could meet some of the staff, and he was coming to us after dark."

"You were pleased?" Úna asked.

"Pleased isn't the word for it," she answered, "but didn't mother begin shaking with the fright. 'God help us, Brian,' says she, 'how do you know the murder-gang wouldn't track him? . . . He to be took in this house . . . Brian,' says she,

'I'd sooner see yourself slaughtered before my eyes! If the Chief's lost, Ireland's lost!' she says.

" 'Is it that you'll refuse to take him, Mother?' says Brian, very quiet-like, and with that she set to work. He was not to be in the house at all, Brian said, for fear of anyone looking in; so we readied up the loft of the barn. Fine and comfortable we made it, working like three fire-engines till the set of sun. We had it fixed up with a bed and table for his writing and a stove and all, and when everything was done we brought in the Sacred Heart picture and made up an altar and said a prayer that he'd be saved and guarded from all harm. Brian was delighted, his blue eyes were dancing in his head and he planning and fixing the place as if for a year. He was pleased you know, that they'd put that much trust in us, to let us mind the Chief. A happy day we had, thanks be to God!

"Well, by the time we had our tea over and I'd done baking and cleaning the house and put a tray ready for his supper when he'd come, it was very late, but mother wouldn't hear of going to bed, so the three of us sat talking round the fire. The plan was that about midnight Brian'd go down to the bridge at the bottom of the bohereen and wait, and about one o'clock the Chief would come that way with a couple of guards and they'd turn back and Brian'd bring him up and they'd go straight into the barn. And the others that were coming to see him in the morning would be disguised as tinkers and labouring men.

"I couldn't make out what ailed mother; she used generally be easy-minded about the house; 'twas so quiet and safe; Brian got downright vexed with her fears. 'If the Chief comes to harm and he in my charge,' he said, 'I'll get you to cut my throat! Don't you think I have my plans made? Or am I a babbler or a fool or a traitor that I'd lead him into a trap? The rest'll do their part,' says he, 'and I'll do mine, with the help of God, and the Chief's safe.'

" 'With the help of God,' mother said then, and she got very patient and quiet. Then to make all happy again Brian began chatting to her and remembering old times. 'Do you mind, Mother,' says he, laughing, 'when I was a gorsoon and I used to be playing tricks on you and my Da, and mitching school? And you used to be saying, "Mind what you're at now, for God's looking at you, if I'm not!" Well, that's the way I do feel sometimes about the Chief, and he not in it at all—you couldn't do a mean or a dirty thing. Whatever misfortunes we get, while he's living we'll get no disgrace.'

"He got up then and took his cap, though 'twas only half eleven and 'twas a wet night. 'I'll scout round a bit,' he said, 'and see are the others at their posts before I go to the bridge.'

"A queer feeling came over me when I saw him taking down his cap, 'Whist,' I said, and he looked at me, wondering, and I said, more for an excuse than anything—'I thought I heard a lorry below on the road.' So we stopped, listening, and I thought I heard it again, but he heard nothing at all. It upset mother though and her face was white. 'Ah, Mother darling!' says he, in the sudden, loving way he had, like a child, 'You'll be the proud woman tomorrow, though 'tis a silly old worrier you are tonight,' and he gave her a hug and a kiss and went off. But two minutes later I heard him tapping at the window and there he was with the lamplight on his face and his black hair wet with the rain. 'Pull the curtain and put out the lamp,' he said, 'for fear anyone'd wonder at the light, and whatever happens,' says he, 'don't look out. Don't be worrying now, but pray for us,' he said.

"He went off then and I did what he told me and we sat by the fire, quiet, a long time.

"The quiet preyed on me and the waiting and I could see mother was terrible anxious, so the two of us knelt down and said the whole rosary for the safety of the Chief.

When we were at the last mystery, the clock struck one and we stopped to listen, but there was not a sound. Then we finished the Rosary and stood up. I began making up the fire, but mother said suddenly, in a kind of whisper, 'Listen, now listen!' She was standing stiff in the middle of the floor. I don't know what she had heard, but I know what I heard then—two shots close to us, sharp and clear, and then two more.

"Mother cried out and fell down on her knees by the chair. I didn't hear another sound. The thoughts were racing one another through my mind—mother was gasping and moaning to herself: 'God have mercy on us, the boy is destroyed and broken!' she said, 'Ireland is lost forever, and we'll be cursed and shamed in the grave!'

" 'What are you saying, Mother?' I whispered to her, and I shaking at her talk.

" 'The Chief is murdered under his protection,' she went on moaning, 'and Brian'll die of shame.'

"I tell you the world went black before my eyes and she saying it. I clutched hold of the curtains; I nearly fell. Then I heard the tapping at the window the same as before, and it put the heart across me till I heard Brian's voice, whispering and gasping, full of dread, 'The bridge, quick, quick!' it said. 'For God's sake, quick, quick, to the bridge!'

" 'Brian's outside, wounded, Mother,' I said, but I ran out myself on to the road, not stopping to look for him, left or right. I had one thought only in my mind—the Chief lying in his blood—I ran down into the bohereen.

"A black night it was, under those twisted trees and neither moon nor stars in the sky. I was running on, the heart threshing within me like a machine, till I came in sight of the bottom of the bohereen and the turn of the road that goes on to the bridge. I was certain sure he was lying there dead. Then something startled me and I stopped—stopped dead, I did, and crouched down in the ditch, and then I saw what it was. I saw men moving, quick and quiet, not a whisper out of them, behind the trees; one after another they lay down, flat on their faces, their rifles levelled on the road and when the last was down there was not a sight nor sign of them—you'd think the road was safe and clear.

"The terror that fell on me was awful. I knew those'd shoot at a shadow; those'd kill a woman as easy as they'd kill a dog . . . I thought I'd never move hand or foot again till the world's end. Then all of a sudden the understanding rushed on me—what it meant, like Heaven opening over a lost soul. I knew they hadn't killed the Chief; they were waiting for him; he hadn't come. 'Quick, quick, quick,' I heard it then, Brian whispering in my heart, and the thought came to me what to do. Out into the middle of the bohereen I went, staggering and singing and talking like a drunk woman to myself. Quite slowly I went past them, reeling from one side to another of the road; just as I turned the corner I heard one of them smothering a laugh. I near laughed myself with the lightness and triumph in my heart. But when I turned the corner, out of sight, I ran . . . O God, the way I ran to the bridge! When I got to it I was dizzy. I'd have fallen, but a man caught me by the arm.

" 'Steady,' he said in a whisper, holding me, and another came up from the far side of the road.

" 'Who are you?' said the first, and the other said, " ' 'Tis Brian's sister. Where's Brian?' he said.

"I could hardly speak, I said just, 'He sent me to the bridge . . . the bohereen's swarming . . . military' . . . but he understood. 'Twas Mick Brady: I knew him well. The other said in a sharp voice, 'Turn back,' and they left me without a word. I ran after Mick and caught him and said, 'Is the Chief safe?' 'He is,' said Mick and the other said, 'Tell Brian he did his work well.'

"I went home by the back way over the fields, slowly, I was tired—so tired I forgot about Brian being wounded up at the house; too happy I was, altogether . . .

"When I got back the men were raging all over the house, plain clothes men and Black and Tans. Mother was standing in the kitchen, her face terrible white, but she was trying not to let them see she was upset.

"They were shouting to one another with voices that'd sicken you, and using awful words. They let me in and stood round me, bullying, showing their revolvers, asking where were the men. I told them, 'You'll get no men here.' They were smashing open cupboards and ripping up mattresses, flinging things about, tearing up the boards—Mother watched them, not saying a word; she was brave.

" 'Is he safe?' she whispered to me when she got a chance. 'He is, thank God,' I said. 'God be praised!' says she: 'What matter now if they burn the house.' 'And where's Brian?' I asked her and she told me she didn't know; he wasn't outside.

"Then the men found the room in the barn and started shouting and got petrol and set fire to it and come throwing petrol about the house.

" 'Come on!' says Mother to me, gathering up some clothes only, and I put on my shawl.

" 'Will you not leave out the bits of furniture?' I said to one of the men.

"He swore. He swore the way you wouldn't swear at a brute beast and said it was more than we deserved if he let us out ourselves.

" 'Go out of that door now!' he shouted, 'and go to Hell, you . . . ' Ah, I wouldn't soil my tongue with the words he used.

" 'You're welcome to the house,' my Mother answered back to him. 'You haven't got Ireland yet.'

"That maddened him and he came down the bohereen yelling after us. 'If you want your son, I'll tell you where to look for him!' he shouted, and we stopped at that.

" 'Where is he?' Mother said to him, so quiet that he got ashamed.

" 'Try under the bridge,' he said, and went back to the house.

"A great blaze the house made by that time and in the light of it we got quick enough down the bohereen. There wasn't a soul on the road or at the bridge itself. We went down the slippery bank into the dark under it, calling, but there was no answer at all.

"We got his body half in and half out of the water. He had four bullets in the chest."

She paused a little; none of us spoke; then she looked up at me.

"The people of the next farm came looking for us with a cart," she said, "and they took up the body and took us home. They were very good."

"Your Mother . . . Your Mother?" Úna asked in a stifled voice.

"She didn't seem to fret too much," Nannie answered: "You see, she'd been prepared for worse. She would keep on saying, 'He did his work well, by God's mercy; he did his work well.' But she died on me before the month was out."

Mountjoy, Christmas Eve.

The Portrait of Róisín Dhu
(FOR S.H.)

It was a year after the artist was drowned that the loan exhibition of Hugo Blake's paintings was opened in Philadelphia by Maeve. "Whom the gods love die young," people said.

To remember those paintings is like remembering a dream-life spent with the Ever-living in an Ireland untrodden by men.

Except once he never painted a human face or any form of life, human or faery, yet the very light and air of them thrilled with life—it was as though he had painted life itself. There was the great *Sliav Gullion*—stony, austere—the naked mountain against the northern sky, and to look at it was to be filled with a young, fierce hunger for heroic deeds, with the might of Cúchulainn and Fionn. There was *Loch Corrib* like a mirage from the first day of Creation—there was Úna's *Dawn* . . .

The critics, inarticulate with wonder, made meaningless phrases: "Blake paints as a seer", "He paints on the astral plane".

At the end of the room, alone on a grey wall, hung the *Portrait of Róisín Dhu*. Before her, Irish men and women stood worshipping, the old with tears, the young with fire in their eyes. There were men whom it sent home.

Had Blake seen, anywhere on earth, others were asking, that heart-breaking, entrancing face? Knowledge of the secrets of God was in the eyes; on the lips was the memory, the endurance and the fore-knowledge of endless pain; yet from the luminous, serene face shone out a beauty that made one crave for the spaces beyond death.

No woman in the world, we said, had been Hugo's Róisín Dhu; no mortal face had troubled him when he painted that immortal dream—that ecstasy beyond fear, that splendour beyond anguish—that wild, sweet holiness of Ireland for which men die.

Maeve, as we knew, had been his only friend. When strangers clamoured, "Was there a woman?" she would not tell. But one evening when we were five only around Úna's fire she told us the strange, incredible tale.

"I will not tell everyone for a while," she said, "because so few would understand, and Hugo, unless one understood to the heights and depths, might seem to have been . . . unkind. But I will tell you: There was a girl."

"It is almost impossible to believe," Liam said; "It is not a human body he has painted; nor even a human soul!"

"That is true in a way," Maeve answered, hesitating; "I will try to make you understand.

"He was the loneliest being I have ever known. He was a little atom of misery and rebellion when my godmother rescued him in France. She bought the child from a drunkard who was starving him almost to death. His mother, you know, was Nora Raftery, the actress; she ran away from her husband with François Raoul, taking the child, and died. Poor Blake rode over a precipice while hunting—mad with grief, and the boy was left without a friend in the world. It was I who taught him to read and write: already he could draw.

"To the end he was the same passionate, lonely child. The anguish of pity and love he had had for his mother he gave to her country when he came home: he suffered unbearable "*heim-weh*" all the years he was studying abroad. The "Dark Tower" as we called it, of our godmother's house on Loch Corrib was the place he loved best.

"I have known no one who lived in such extremes, always, of misery or of joy. In any medium but paint he was helpless—chaotic or dumb, yet I think that his pictures came to him first not visually at all, but as intense perceptions of a mood. And between that moment of perception and the moment when it took form and colour in his mind he used to be like a wild creature in pain. He would prowl day and night around the region he meant to paint, waiting in a rage of impatience for the right moment of light and shadow to come, the incarnation of the soul . . . Then, when he had found it, the blessed mood of contentment would come and he would paint, day after day, until it was done. At those times, in the evenings, he would be exhausted and friendly and grateful like a child.

"For all the vehemence that you feel in his work he painted very slowly, with intense, exquisite care, like a man in love. That is indeed what he was,—in love, obliviously, with whatever spirit had enthralled his imagination at the time. And when the picture was finished and the vision gone he fell into a mood of desolation in which he wanted to die. He was very young.

"I tried to scold Hugo out of those moods. I was with him in April just after he had finished his *Loch Corrib*—you know the innocence, the angelic tranquillity in it, like the soul of a child. He would not go near the lake: 'It is nothing to me now,' he said sombrely, 'I have done with it.'

" 'Hugo!' I said, laughing, 'you are a vampire! The loch has given you its soul.' He answered, 'Yes: that is true; corpses are ugly things.'

"For a month that empty, dead mood lasted and Hugo hated all the world. I took him to London to give him something to hate. After two days he fled back to his tower and breathed the smell of the peat and sea-wind, and the sweet, home-welcome of burning turf, and looked out on Ireland with eyes of love. The next morning he came in from a bathe in the loch with the awakened, wondering look I had longed to see and said, 'I am going to paint Róisín Dhu.' Then he went off to walk the west of Ireland seeking a woman for his need.

"I was astonished and excited beyond words; he had been so contemptuous of human subjects, although I remembered, in his student days, studies for heads and hands that had made one artist whisper, 'Leonardo!' under his breath.

"I wondered what woman he would bring home.

"They came about two weeks later, after dark, rowing over the loch, Hugo and the girl alone.

"After supper, sitting over the turf fire in the round hall of the tower, Hugo told me that she was the daughter of a king.

"She smiled at him, knowing that he spoke of her although she had no English at all, and I told her in Irish what he had said. She answered gravely, 'It is true.'

"I looked at her then as she moved from the window to her chair, and I felt almost afraid—her beauty was so delicate and so remote . . .

" 'Those red lips with all their mournful pride' . . . Poems of Yeats were haunting me while I looked at her. But it was the beauty of one asleep, unaware of life or of sorrow or of love . . . the . . . face of a woman whose light is hidden . . .

"She sat in the shadowed corner, brooding, while Hugo talked. He was at his happiest, overflowing with childish delight in his achievement and with eagerness for tomorrow's sun.

"Nuala was her name. The King of the Blasket Isles was her father—a superstitious, tyrannical old man. Hugo had been able to make no way with him or his sons.

" 'I invited one of them to come too, and take care of her,' he said, 'but they would not hear of it at all.

" 'The old man was as dignified as a Spanish Grandee.

" ' "It is not that I would be misdoubting you, honest man," says he, "but my daughter is my daughter and there is no call for her to be going abroad to the world."

" 'And her brothers was as obstinate:

" ' " 'Tis not good to be put in a picture: it takes from you," they said.

" 'They got me into a boat by a ruse, rowed me "back to Ireland" and when they had landed me pulled off.

" ' "The blessing of God on your far travelling!" they called to me gravely: a hint that I would not be welcome to the island again.

" 'You can imagine the frenzy I was in!' he said. And I could, well. He had walked night after night on the rocks of the mainland planning some desperate thing, but one night Nuala came to him, rowed out through the darkness by some boys who braved the vengeance of the old king for her sake. He rewarded them extravagantly and brought Nuala home.

"He told it all triumphantly, and Nuala looked up at him from time to time with a gentle gaze full of content and rest. But my heart sank: there was only one possible end to this; Hugo, at his best, was loving and kind and selfless—all might be well—but I knew my Hugo after work.

"She slept in my room and talked to me, softly, in the dark, asking me questions about Hugo's work. 'He told me you were his sister-friend,' she said.

"I told her about his childhood, his suffering and his genius: she listened and sighed.

" 'It is a pity of him to be so long lonely,' she said, 'but he will not be lonely any more.'

" 'Why, Nuala?' I asked, my heart heavy with dread for her. Her answer left me silent.

" 'I myself will be giving him love.'

"Hugo had found a being as lost to the world as himself. How would it end for her, I wondered. She slept peacefully, but I lay long awake.

"The next morning work began in the studio at the top of the tower. I gave up all thought of going home. Nuala would need me.

"Hugo was working faster than usual it seemed, beginning as soon as the light was clear and never pausing until it failed. I marvelled at Nuala's endurance, but I dared not plead for her. I had wrecked a picture of Hugo's once by going into his studio while he painted: his vision fled from him at the least intrusion and I had learned to keep aloof.

"Day after day, when they came down at last to rest and eat, I could measure his progress by the sombre glow of power in his eyes. I could imagine some young druid when his spells proved potent, looking like that.

"But the change that came over Nuala frightened me; he was wearing her away: her face had a clear, luminous look, her eyes were large and dark; I saw an expression in them sometimes as of one gazing into an abyss of pain. The change that might come to a lovely woman in years, seemed to come to her in days: the beauty of her, as she sat in the candle-light, gazing at her own thoughts in the shadows, would still your breathing. It grew more wonderful, more tragic, from day to day.

"One night after she had stolen away to bed, exhausted, while Hugo sat by the fire in a kind of trance, I forced myself to question him.

" 'Hugo,' I said, as lightly as I could, with my heart throbbing: 'Is it that you are in love with your Róisín Dhu?'

"He looked up suddenly, with a dark fire in his eyes. 'Love,' he whispered in a voice aching with passion. He rose and threw back his head and cried out in tones like deep music—

" 'I could plough the blue air!
I could climb the high hills!
    O, I could kneel all night in prayer
To heal your many ills!'

"Then he sighed and went away.

"Nuala's look was becoming, day by day, a look of endurance and resignation that I could not bear, as of one despairing of all human happiness yet serene.

"At last I questioned him again:

" 'Will you be marrying your Róisín Dhu?'

"He turned on me startled, with a laugh, both angry and amazed.

" 'What a question! What an outrageous question, Maeve!'

"I was unanswered still.

"When seven weeks had gone I grew gravely anxious. I feared that Nuala would die: she had the beauty you could imagine in a spirit new-awakened from death, a look of anguish and ecstasy in one . . . She was frail and spent; she scarcely spoke to me or seemed to know me; she slept always in the garden alone.

"It was towards the end of June that I said to Hugo, 'You are wearing your model out.'

" 'I am painting her better than God created her,' he answered. Then he said, contentedly, 'I shall have done with her very soon.'

"I cannot express the dread that fell on me then; I was torn with irresolution. To interfere with Hugo—to break the spell of his vision, would not only sacrifice the picture, it might destroy him. I thought his reason would not survive the laceration, the passion that would follow the shattering of that dream.

"That night I found Nuala utterly changed. She came down from the studio dull-eyed and ugly and went straight to bed in my room.

"Hugo told me he did not want her any more.

"I rowed her out next morning across the loch: it was one of those grey, misty days when it is loveliest; the Twelve Bens in the distance looked like mountains of Hy Breasail, the weeds and sedges glimmering silvery-gold . . . but she had no eyes for its beauty, no beauty of her own, no light . . . she lay drowsy and unresponsive on her cushions; her hands and face were like wax.

"I would have rebelled that night, taken any risk, to make Hugo undo what he had done. She lay down to sleep under a willow by the water's edge and I went to him in the hall. He was standing by the fire and turned to me as I came in; there was a look of wondering humility in his face, as if his own achievement were a thing to worship—a thing he could not understand.

" 'Tomorrow!' he said: 'It will be finished in an hour: you shall see it.' Then he came and took my hands in his old, affectionate way and said:

" 'You have been such a good sister-friend!' One hour more! She must endure it: I would not sacrifice him for that. But I lay awake all night oppressed with a sense of fear and cruelty and guilt.

"At breakfast time there was no Hugo: he had eaten and started work. Old Kate rang the bell in the garden but Nuala did not come. My fears had vanished with the sweet air and sunshine of the early morning: larks were singing; it was mid-June: the joy of Hugo's triumph was my own joy. I went down to the willow where I had left Nuala asleep. She was lying there still; she never stirred when I touched her. She was cold.

"I called no one, I ran madly up the spiral stair to Hugo's studio in the tower. Outside his door I paused: the memory of the last time I had broken in and the devastating consequences arrested me even then. I pushed the door open without a sound and stood inside, transfixed.

"I looked for a moment and grew dizzy, so amazing was the thing I saw. Hugo stood by his easel: before him on the dais, glimmering in the misty silver light, stood Nuala, gazing at him, all a radiance of consummated sacrifice and sweet, unconquerable love—Nuala, as you have seen her in the portrait of Róisín Dhu.

"Hugo stumbled, laid down his brush, drew his hand over his eyes, then turned and, seeing me, said, 'It is done.'

"When I looked again at the dais she was gone. I was shaken to the heart with fear. I cried out, 'Come to her! She is dead.'

"He ran with me down to the water's edge.

"I believe I had hoped that he would be able to waken her, but she was cold and dead, lying with wide-open eyes.

"Hugo knelt down and touched her, then rose quickly and turned away: 'How unbeautiful!' he said.

"I called out to him sternly, angrily, and he looked down at her again, then stooped and lifted her in his arms.

" 'Maeve, Maeve!' he cried then, piteously: 'Have I done this?'

"He brought her home with state to the Island, told them she had been his bride and gave her such a burial as the old King's heart approved. Then he came home again to his lonely house. I left it before he came; he had told me he wanted to be alone.

"I heard nothing of him then for a long time and felt uneasy and afraid. After I had written many anxious letters a strange, disjointed answer came.

" 'She has never left me,' he wrote. 'She is waiting, near, quite near. But what can I do? This imprisoning body—this suffocating life—this burdenous mortality—this dead world.

" 'The picture is for you, sister-friend, and for Ireland when you die.'

"Before I could go to him the picture came and with it the news that he was drowned.

"They found the boat far out on the loch."

Maeve's face was pale when she ended: she covered her eyes for a moment with her hand.

"He had seen the hidden vision . . . " one of us said.

Nesta was looking into the fire, her dark eyes wide with foreboding.

"It is written in Destiny," she said: "the lovers of Róisín Dhu must die."

A Story Without an End
(FOR N.C.)

I t was soon after the truce began that Nesta McAllister came to Philadelphia. A little shyly she came among us and a little critically she was received; many of us had worked with Roger McAllister and delighted in him as the wittiest, believed in him as the most creative and inspiring of Ireland's men, and we wondered, when we heard of his marriage, whether he had been lucky and wise.

We liked Nesta; very young, very dark, she was, very serious at times, without the defiant gaiety that is the only armour for such a war as she had to wage.

She contributed little to the talk and storytelling of those evenings, but loved to listen, and one felt in her a sensitive response to one's precise meaning, one's more discriminate thought, which made the talk grow subtler when she was there. Úna, who knew her best, said of her: "She has lost herself in Roger's life and mind." Frank said: "She is a little woman who'll get hurt."

It was on one evening when we had been recalling old prophecies and forebodings and telling of omens and dreams that she told us her troubling story; she told it, I think, chiefly to hear us assure her that the dream could never come true.

It had happened in January when she and Roger were living in hiding in the mountains of County Cork, he waging with his pen a campaign so dangerous to the enemy and so infuriating that we dreaded capture for him more than death. No man in Ireland was more remorselessly hunted then.

"It was in the middle of the worst time of all," she said, "when martial law had been proclaimed and men were being tried by drum-head Court-Martial and shot on any pretext at all. You could be shot for 'harbouring rebels', you know. We didn't harbour rebels, of course, because Roger's work had all to be done 'underground'; we lived without even a servant in a little four-roomed cottage in the hills. When it was necessary for Roger to meet the staff he used to go off alone on his bicycle at night and come back just when there came a chance. Those, of course, were my worst times.

"It was on a night when he was away that I had the dream. You know," she said, hesitating a little, "that I have had dreams sometimes that came true. I dreamed of my father's stroke, though he was quite well, just before it came—I saw his face change—and my sister's baby—before it was born. I saw it under the sea—and afterwards, in the Leinster, they were both drowned. It is terrible to dream like that.

"As a rule when Roger was away I couldn't sleep, but that night I was very tired and fell asleep before twelve o'clock. In the dream we were sitting, he and I, in a room lighted only by candles—the living-room of the cottage it was—I saw the make-shift couch by the fire and the door that opened straight on to the road. It was night; the door and shutters were bolted and there was no sound. I think I was looking into the fire—I was looking at something, anyhow, that shaped itself into a face—a thin, long face with hollow eyes. I hated it, I tried to drive it away. Then we were in the room, just as before, Roger writing by the candle-light, with no sound—I was waiting for a sound.

Then it came—footsteps on the gravel outside, and a long, low, hissing call, then a knock, someone knocking with his knuckles on the door. Roger stood up and crossed the room quickly and opened the door and four men carrying a stretcher came in; they came walking slowly like figures in a play; there was a man lying on the stretcher—a dead man, with that long, thin face and those deep eyes; there was a blood-stained bandage round his head—I hated him—I was afraid—such terror gripped me that I woke. I woke cold and shuddering, but I didn't wake properly. I fell asleep again and then—then came the other dream."

Her face had gone white and her eyes wide and dark. "Better not be telling it," Frank said. But she crushed her hands together and said, "No, no—I'll get rid of it—'tis better for me to tell."

"In this dream I was not present myself—I knew in a way that I was asleep—there was a mad feeling that if only I could wake—if only I could cry out—but I had no power.

"There were high stone walls and a dark yard; everything was cold; it was dawn. The yard was full of stones; it was narrow and long; there was a dark hole dug in the earth. There was a man standing near it, against the wall; his hands were behind his back and his eyes were bandaged; there was a bright red mark over his heart. It was Roger; he was going to be killed. Soldiers formed up with rifles and stood covering him. There were nine; I counted them; it was all quite clear. Then a tall man stood behind them, an officer, with a revolver, covering them. I looked at him and tried to scream—I tried to stop him, but I couldn't, I had no power. He was the dead man—he had a great scar on his brow and hollow eyes, and that long, cadaverous face. I heard him shout 'Fire!' and heard the volley, and saw Roger fall, and saw that man go over to him with his revolver and shoot—Oh, it was horrible. I can't."

79

She broke off. For a while none of us could think of anything to say, then Liam Daly said laughingly, "One of the uncounted terrors of martial law! I suppose our misfortunate wives and mothers were dreaming our executions every night! God pity them," he added soberly, "the time they had."

Nesta looked up gratefully. "Yes, it was very natural," she said, "and there was one thing that showed how it was—just a crazy combination of hopes and fears. The uniforms of the soldiers were *green*! That comforted me, of course, but the first part of the dream came true."

"The wounded man?" I exclaimed.

"That evening," she said, "Roger came home. He was in splendid spirits; everything was going well; one man who'd been sentenced was reprieved, and another who was to have been executed in the morning had escaped. We had a leisurely supper and afterwards sat resting by the firelight, as usual, before beginning the night's work. You know Roger," she said smiling: "One resolves to conceal things from him, but it's no good. In a few minutes I was telling him my dream. He knew, of course, that I had dreamed things that came true, and when I came to the execution he looked startled until I told him "the soldiers were in green".

" 'In green!' he exclaimed. 'In the uniform of the I. R. A.?' and I said, 'Yes.' Then he laughed and began inventing nonsense, delightedly—'Victory for the Republic,' he said, 'our army all swank in uniform and me charged with high treason and shot at dawn!' It was so absurd that the whole dread that had been over me fell away and I laughed too, and we lit the lamps and pulled out the files and papers and began work.

"We both loved, for writing, the unbroken quiet of the midnight hours, and we worked in dead silence until after one o'clock; then the lamp began to flicker out, and Roger muttered, 'Sorry, I forgot the oil,' so I had to light candles.

"It was that, I suppose—the candles—that brought it back—the face out of my dream—suddenly I saw it before me in the shadows, ghastly clear, and my heart crumpled up with dread. I sat down at the table again, trying not to tell Roger, waiting—but I couldn't work, couldn't think.

"At last it came, a sound of slow footsteps on the gravel and a long low, hissing call. Roger sprang up instinctively and opened the drawer in which he kept his automatic, but then the knock came—someone knocking with his knuckles—and he put it back and crossed to open the door.

"I cried out and stood against the door. I cried out to him, 'Don't open, don't open!' He put his arm around me and drew me away, smiling. 'It isn't raiders,' he said.

He flung the door open and they came in, four men in dark coats, walking slowly, and laid the stretcher down. I saw the white face of the man who lay on it, the long, lean, hollow face—the bandaged head—the blood—Oh, I was not brave; I could do nothing; I sank down on a chair in the shadow and did nothing at all. I heard the men whispering with Roger and heard them go away. They had laid the man on the couch, and he was moaning—that was the dreadful thing—he was not dead.

"Roger came over to me, smiling. 'Nesta, we've got to harbour a rebel,' he said. He said that to call up my courage, of course, and it did make me ashamed. I stood up and went to the couch; then I looked at Roger and told him, 'It's the face in my dream.' 'This boy was to be executed tomorrow,' he said gravely. 'It was a great rescue: he was fired after and hit; it's a bad wound, but I think he needn't die.' I—I couldn't help it—I said again, stupidly, 'It's the face in my dream.' Roger looked at me almost—he was almost stern—and said, 'Nesta, we can't let dreams—' I took off the bandage then and examined the wound; it wasn't dangerous, only he'd lost so much blood; he'd need long, careful nursing I could see; but he needn't die. He was five weeks in the house."

"Tell me, did you like him?" Úna asked. "No," Nesta said, frankly. "Roger did. Roger said he was a splendid fellow with a fine record since nineteen sixteen—one of Mick Collins's right-hand men. But I—I was ashamed—I could see nothing to hate, yet I—I hated him. But I did my best, he went away strong and well."

"And that's the end of the story," Liam said.

"Yes, that's the end," said Nesta, looking up. "You see— the war will break out again of course, we all know that— but the green uniforms—it couldn't come true."

Mountjoy, December, 1922.

On Leaving Mountjoy

We shall remember it with pride
Who pass this bitter gate where waves
The captive flag o'er captive graves;
We lived where those, our noblest, died.

January 1923.

Escape

It was ten when Father Kiernan went to the gaol; it was going on for midnight now; with a sound that was like the death-watch, time ticked on. There was no sound in the world but that ticking, and the shuddering breathing of the child. The fit of terror and crying had left her lifeless; she lay with her eyes closed and her lips parted, her hands, palms upward, spread out on the counter pane. With her little face worn and peaked from suffering and her dark head shorn like a boy's she had a queer look of Festy now.

The priest was a long time gone; it took but eight minutes to the gaol; he was kept there, surely—waiting to bring the boy . . .

Mrs. Fahy went to the crib and lit the candles. They shone on the gold of the picture of Our Lady of Perpetual Succour, every one a prayer. It was a beautiful crib and it took up the whole of the top of the chest of drawers. It would be the first thing Nora would see when her eyes opened—it would distract her, maybe, from her terror and her crying for Festy, for a while.

If only they could have kept it from her that this was Christmas Eve! But every night, since fifty nights ago when he was taken, even in her illness, she had marked off the days on the almanac on the wall. She had it under her pillow now.

"Don't fret, Noreen *a gradh*," he had said to her, leaning down to her from the lorry; "I'll come home to you for Christmas, never fear."

'Twas a pity he ever said it, he that never broke a promise to Nora yet. Day long the sick child had been listening and watching for him, till by evening she was burning with fever again. Then the fit of delirium and raving terror, the wild screams that they were willing Festy, killing him the way they had killed Shawn . . . Father Kiernan quieted her at last, saying it would not be Christmas till midnight, and maybe at midnight Festy would come. Then he had gone, to plead in Christ's name, to the gaol.

John was sitting crouched over the hearth; the trouble was turning him into an old man. His wife sat down by him and put turf on the fire.

"She is lying very quiet," she whispered. "If he comes now, please God, she'll get well."

John did not look up; he said, heavily, "He'll not come."

"They'll hardly refuse the priest," she said, "and it Christmas night!"

" 'Twas on the feast of the Immaculate Conception," he answered, "they did their murders in Mountjoy."

Her faith battled with his bitterness: "The Mother of God will put pity in their hearts this night, surely, for the sake of her Holy Child."

Her husband was not listening; he was muttering to himself.

"God knows I never grudged the boys to Ireland. I never lifted a word against Him when they slaughtered Shawn. Why wouldn't he leave the little girl to me, that is the light and angel of my days?"

Her man was crying and she could not comfort him. She sat silent, listening to the passing of life and time.

ɛ∂

Father Kiernan sat facing the Governor at the office table. The business-like room with its filing cabinets, documents tied with red tape and printed schedules, drained him of his confidence. His mission began to appear like a pitiful effort to stay the ruthless wheels of some huge machine. But he noticed that holly and ivy were twined round the gas-jet and that gave him hope.

The Governor, a stout man with a pale, somnolent face, listened to him in silence, pricking a paper with a pencil all the time.

"I remember the case of Shawn Fahy," he said at last. "Shot while trying to escape, wasn't he, by the Black and Tans?"

"They dragged him from the house at night . . . Only his mother and little Nora were in it . . . They heard the shots . . . Some friends brought the body in . . . The little girl was in convulsions all night . . . She has never got over it. There is only herself and Festy left, and when your men took Festy away . . ."

At the Governor's impatient gesture Father Kiernan broke off.

"He was identified as taking part in the attack on the barracks. Two of my men were killed. A revolver was found in his bed."

Father Kiernan's tone became pleading, shaken by nervousness.

"But the little girl! It's life or death for her to-night. These convulsions of terror would kill a strong man. If her brother doesn't come . . . Another attack—the doctor warned them—it would be the last. To see him, to speak to him for even a few minutes might save her life. Can't you give him one hour's parole? I will be responsible myself. I beg it. I ask it in the name of charity—in the name of Jesus Christ!"

The Governor's pencil tore a gash in his paper, but he spoke in a controlled formal tone:

"The Government cannot grant parole on any grounds whatever. I refused it to a man whose wife was dying only last week. He signed the undertaking, however, and was released in time for the funeral."

Father Kiernan's gentle face looked troubled.

"Festy . . . He was always a determined lad," he said, "but he's crazy about little Nora . . . If it is to save her life . . . I wouldn't like to press him in any way, but still . . . "

The Governor shook his head.

"You don't quite understand the situation," he said. "It is more serious than that. In possession of a revolver—you see? The courtsmartial will be coming on. The penalty, as you know . . . "

"In God's holy name!" Father Kiernan recoiled, paling. "You would not . . . you could not . . . execute . . . ?"

"It has been done in similar cases," was the firm reply. "To be perfectly open with you—I speak in confidence, Father," he continued, "the probability is that this batch of prisoners will be sentenced to death. The sentences would not, however, be carried out unless the Irregulars gave trouble in the area. It would rest with themselves."

"Hostages!" Father Kiernan exclaimed.

The Governor did not reply.

"Have you no compassion for the poor people?" the priest cried out then. "Shawn murdered, little Nora dying, Festy . . . Is there no humanity left in Ireland?"

The Governor considered for a moment, his lips compressed. Then he struck the bell on his table.

"I will send for the prisoner," he said. "Perhaps something can be done. So far I have failed; but if you will add your efforts to mine . . . "

෴

The joy that lit up Festy's face at the sight of Father Kiernan had changed to white, staring anguish when the tale was told.

"Little Nora! Little Nora!" he gasped. "I—I'd give up my life to come to her! What will I do? O my God, what will I do?" His head went down between clenched hands for a moment, then he wheeled and faced the Governor and said abruptly, "You sent for me; what do you want?"

There was a pause. The Governor rose, crossed to the door, locked it, came back to his chair again and lit a cigarette.

"Festy Fahy," he said then, speaking gravely: "You have a duty to your family, haven't you? A little sister dying. Your parents growing old. They have no other son. The courtsmartial come on next month and your case is the most serious that will come before them. I have said nothing to Father Kiernan, but you trust him, I suppose . . . "

Festy's whole body was strung tense, his head set back. He spoke between his teeth, interrupting:

"What is your price?"

The Governor spake slowly, without looking at him: "I made a proposal to you before. The same proposal is open again—for the last time."

Father Kiernan had known Festy Fahy since he was a loving, sunny-hearted little ragamuffin, impossible to approve of and hard to scold. He had never known the boy who stood opposite the Governor now, bent forward, his hands clutching the table, his face distorted, his voice choked with hate.

"You cur! You devil!" the boy gasped out. "Nora's dying and you'd use it to make an informer of me! You play your filthy game with the child's life! O God's curse on your for a murderer!"

Father Kiernan flung his arms round Festy and the boy clung to him, broken down.

" 'Tis a thing I couldn't do! Don't ask me, Father! I couldn't—to save Nora's life!"

The Governor rose again, opened the door and called an orderly.

"Take the prisoner back to his cell," he ordered, "and if he is fit to go to midnight Mass . . . "

Despairing sobs echoed through the dark corridors as Festy was led away. Father Kiernan said "Good-night," and went out into the foggy air. He felt confused. It would be bad, going back alone to the Fahys. He would call home first for the Holy Oils . . .

The prison chapel was lighted up; the prisoners were getting midnight Mass; it was by no means the worst of all gaols.

⁂

Five minutes to twelve and the priest not back yet. Mrs. Fahy got up noiselessly and took down the clock, saying she would put back the hands. Her husband stopped her.

"You can't cheat the child," he said, "and you can't cheat Death. She'll hear the Christmas bells."

Nora was wakeful again and moaning:

"Festy, darling, put your hand on my head—'tis hurting me—can't you stop the pain? . . . where are you, Festy? . . . Mammie, mammie, I want Festy; why doesn't he come?"

John stood at the foot of the bed, impotent, looking down at the child with sombre eyes. The mother sat down, bathing her forehead, murmuring that Festy would come soon, surely—that it wasn't Christmas yet.

The child grew easier then and talked to herself in a soft, contented little voice. "I will hear him coming down the street and the latch will be lifted and I will hear him crossing the kitchen and he will come in at the door. He will be laughing. He will make me well . . . "

They heard footsteps while she whispered to herself and heard the latch lifted, but it was Father Kiernan and he was alone. He stood in the doorway and shook his head sorrowfully. His face was drawn with grief.

The mother and father stood still, saying nothing, while clearly and remorselessly the clock struck twelve. Nora lay stretched out on the bed, gazing up at their stricken faces. Terror was gathering in her eyes; a shrill little cry broke from her and she trembled from head to foot. Outside the bells clashed and clanged, broke into chimes and then into a tune: "Come all ye faithful—". The clamour was pierced by the sharp crack of a shot . . . "Joyful and triumphant!" Another shot crashed out and the bells rang on. A storm was rising round Mrs. Fahy—a blackness drowning her senses; John was saying " 'Tis from the gaol!" and Father Kiernan answered quickly, "No, no! It is nothing. Don't fear, Mrs. Fahy; we'll go and see." The two of them went away. She could not see Nora for the dark fog that was in her eyes. She reached the altar, but the lights slid away from her . . . The room floated away from her and she fell.

∽

When her senses came back to her Nora was calling in a weak, excited voice. Mrs. Fahy rose dizzily and drank some cold water and knelt down by the child's bed. Nora's eyes were wide and wondering: a sweet radiance lit up her face; she was lying quite still.

"Mammie, mammie, didn't you see him?" She asked softly. "Why were you sleeping on the floor? He came so quiet, so quiet, and he couldn't stay. He put his hand on my forehead and the pain is gone."

Mrs. Fahy's heart was beating painfully. She heard people running past the window, no other sound.

"Tell me, daughter, what did he say to you?" she asked under her breath.

Nora was drowsy. "He just said he escaped from them," she replied sleepily. "He said he would be safe from them now: he will be in a place where they can't find him ever, he said, and we are not to be afraid any more."

Her eyelids closed but she opened them to say, "Please, Mammie, go to bed; you are so tired." Then she was fast asleep.

ℰℬ

There were voices at the street door: there were people around the house, whispering; an old man's feet came dragging across the kitchen floor. Mrs. Fahy went in. John was there with the priest. He lifted his face with a half-blind look, speechless, and shook his head slowly from side to side, then sank down in his chair.

She looked at Father Kiernan. The women in the doorway were sobbing but there was calmness in her voice.

"Is it Festy?" she asked.

"God comfort you!" Father Kiernan said, his voice trembling. There were tears in his eyes. He took her by the two hands.

"It is Festy. He collapsed during Mass, it seems, and some of the Guards took him out. Crossing the yard he made a dash for the wall. He had no chance at all and he never reached it. He was shot through the heart."

Mrs. Fahy said nothing for a moment, but looked at him with bewildered eyes. Then: "Aren't God's ways very strange, Father" she said, and turned to her man.

John put up his hands and clung to her. She folded him in her arms.

"Little Nora is spared to us, John," she told him gently. "Come and look at the lovely sleep that is on her. She is spared to us: God is good!"

The Curlew's Cry

'Twould be little use, Mary knew well, trying to sleep, though such tiredness was over her that she could have crept into comforting arms, had there been any to hold her, and cried like a child.

She raked the glowing ashes together on the hearth-stone, turned out the lamp, lit the candle and went into her cold room. But she did not undress. There was a listening wakefulness in her head: her heart throbbed, paining her, and she heard her breath come shudderingly, as though she were afraid. Tears welled, stinging, into her eyes.

The open square of her window showed no star; nothing but thick blackness lay outside; the curlews were crying out, wild and lonesome, over the boglands; the wind was crying shrill along the quarries below; from far off came the low, sorrowful singing of the sea. And in the wide night there was no one stirring—except the soldiers maybe, hunting for men . . .

The harsh crackle of rifle shots split the silence; it must have been near the quarries, it echoed so . . . Godsend they were not raiding the Glen!

She went back to the hearth and sat down again on her stool, striving to gather quietness in her mind. " 'Tis too much!" something inside her was crying, but that was wrong and she answered it, clasping her hands tightly together—"Nothing is too much."

A kind of strong peace came to her then. She rose and opened the door and a sweet, moist air blew in from the night. The world lay dark before her, the ridges of the hills scarcely visible against the heavy, clouded sky. But there was a pale, still glimmer where the sea lay and lights shone in the harbour of Carrigrone. A thought seemed to blow into her mind with the wind. She would be wanted—she would be ready—she would not be long alone. Half in obedience to the whispering thought she put fresh sods on the fire.

She went in then, and knelt praying a long time, and lay down, dressed, on her bed.

&

As far back as memory went of them the Gilligans had lived in that little stone cottage on the mountain. There John Gilligan had been born, and there, in the fullness of time, two strong sons had been born to him, and one daughter, and Tom, the poor weakling boy, whose crippled life had cost the mother her own. The home had seen little, since the fighting started, of Jo and Peader, but John Gilligan would not complain. He had his health yet, thank God, and poor Tom was no fool. And if his own boys were far off, many another man's son got good rest and shelter in it, in those times of peril and dread.

Tom would stay out the long night through watching, and come in at dawn to guide them again on their way, and return, dark and wistful, to the work of the farm. It was Tom who used to be reading to her the old stories and ballads of Owen Roe and Sarsfield and Emmet, since first he had learnt to read: Mary knew, though not a word of it was said between them, how near Tom's heart would be to breaking when the lads fastened their rifle straps in the morning and swung off into the hills

And three nights ago they had taken her father and Tom, surrounding the house noiselessly while all were sleeping and suddenly breaking in. The officer hurt Tom, twisting his arm, asking where the guns were, and she screamed. But in Tom's face when they were taking him away, handcuffed, in the lorry, there was a kind of joy. Her father looked gloomy, though, thinking she would be there alone . . .

"Get Kitty Ryan to sleep with you," he said to her, bending down, and she had promised, but Kitty refused to come. She would go down to Carrigrone tomorrow and see would one of the Timminys come . . .

What harm, anyway, being lonely? There were girls who had worse to bear . . . If only they didn't beat poor Tom. Father had never beaten him, ever, even the day he took the pony out on the road and it ran away—laughing, Tom was, too, the villain, with his little thin face and big eyes—laughing, and he crossed the stepping stones on his crutches—running on his crutches to her . . . Tap, tap, tap . . .

☙

Mary sprang up, startled. Someone was knocking at the door—knocking lightly—'twas not a raid . . . With a head still mazed with dream she crossed and opened it, and bolted it quickly behind the man who stepped in.

Very tall, he seemed, in the darkness of the little porch. Mary could not see his face. He spoke in a deep voice hushed to a whisper. "Is this John Gilligan's? Did Andy Timminy call? A lad belonging to Carrigrone."

"No," Mary replied, wondering. "Andy didn't come."

The stranger seemed perplexed.

"Did he not? He had an hour's start of me. He was to warn you that I'd be here. I hope nothing went wrong . . . "

He seemed lost in thought for a moment, then spoke contentedly: "Anyway, he gave me good instructions; I

96

found my way. He said surely your father would take me in. Niell O'Lochlawn is my name."

"You are welcome, Niell O'Lochlawn," Mary replied gravely. "Your name is well known to us here. Won't you rest yourself by the fire?"

A little flush had come to her pale face. Niell O'Lochlawn! The man Tom would be talking about day in, day out, comparing him to heroes of old times! It was Niell O'Lochlawn rescued the men in Scotland who were being taken to Peterhead. It was he broke out of jail when he was sentenced to execution and got captured trying to carry Andy, because Andy had a wounded leg, and escaped again . . . It was he took Drumcarn Castle with seven men . . . His was a name of power.

She was too busy to talk, putting eggs in the pan, pushing gorse-bushes under the pot, setting the table for a meal; and he, too, was silent, sitting forward in her father's chair, his head on his right hand.

It was not until she knelt by him to blow up the fire that she noticed dark stains on his left sleeve.

"You're not wounded?" she exclaimed.

He drew his hand out of his pocket and looked at it.

"Only a graze; it's bleeding all the time, though. It made me weak. Maybe if you have a rag . . . ?"

While Mary got warm water and linen and bandaged the injured hand he told her, with keen enjoyment, the story of his escape, his brown, furrowed face and dark eyes lit up by the leaping fire.

"A 'poteen still' we had in the old limekiln away there in Ben Ro, but 'twas something stronger than poteen! High explosives—Celignite. We must have been informed on, I think. They surrounded us at dark and thought they had us trapped like badgers, but we fought them for one good hour and every one of us got away. I think none of the rest were hurt . . . Thank you, that's splendid now!"

"Are they after you?" Mary asked anxiously. "You're worn out . . . Do they know which direction you took at all?"

"I think not. Andy guided me by some twisted way of his own. He's the best boy in the world. He stuck to me like a brother, though he was good for twice my pace. I got weak from loss of blood. I made him go ahead then, to prepare you and get on to Carrigrone before daylight. I was to give three whistles like a curlew if I got lost or needed help. It is a signal we had. His plan is to go to Carrigrone and arrange for a boat to take us to the Island tomorrow night. Meanwhile I might stay here . . . But isn't your father? . . . Surely you're not alone?"

He stood up and looked at the frail girl before him with compassion gathering in his eyes. She *was* alone, he could see it before she answered—the loneliest little soul in the world.

She lifted grey eyes to his face calmly: "Tom and father were taken on Friday night," she said; "I think you'll be safe here for a while."

Without answering he sat down to supper, Mary waiting on him briefly. She felt no uneasiness, he could see; if he had been her own brother returned she would not have shown a more serene, happy countenance in sheltering him.

A great surge of desire—desire for life, that he had held so lightly—for all the tranquil years that might be, rose in him. It was weakening: he fought it down.

"Your father—he wouldn't mind? . . . No one would be vexed with you for keeping me?" he asked gently.

"My father would not forgive me," she answered, "if I turned any hunted rebel from this door."

"I will stay, so, and God bless you." he said, smiling.

A thought held Mary very still.

"If they caught you," she said in a low voice, "they would kill you, wouldn't they?"

He laughed. "Oh, they have a rope in pickle for me right enough but they're not going to take me alive . . . "

He stopped, reproaching himself; what a child she was, with her fair, silky hair and pale, little trustful face! But she met his look with a smile.

"Andy'll get you safe away," she said, "if anyone will. I know Andy; he used to be helping Tom."

"Yes, yes," he replied; "I'm sure Andy will do it somehow. He's a brave little lad."

Mary was handing him a lighted candle but it was blown out in his hand. The door had swung open; a sharp, chilling air blew in. Niell turned quickly, his revolver in his hand, facing the night. Mary started to his side and for a moment they stood waiting, tense. Then Mary turned to him with a little gasp, half laughing:

"I was frightened! Wasn't it Andy? Why doesn't he come in?" She went to the door and looked out.

"He is beckoning to you," she whispered. "Something is wrong."

Niell stood behind her in the doorway and looked out. He saw the low stone wall and the shape of a haystack beyond it; nothing else but the strong line of the hills.

"I see no one there," he said.

Mary looked up at him, astonished. "He was behind you in the doorway when it opened. Didn't you see him?"

Niell shook his head with a low laugh. "You are dreaming! There's no one there."

"But look! Look!" She was trembling as her hand clutched his arm. "There, with his hands to his mouth calling! Don't you see the light of his hair?"

Niell drew her in and shut the door.

"Child," he said, "you are tired; you are upset. Go to bed and have a sound sleep till morning. There's not a living soul out there." But her face was white as death and she sprang past him, opening the door again.

"Look there! He has come closer! He is there by the wall! He is calling you!" And she ran out crying in a low anguished voice, "Come in! Come in!"

Niell saw her stumble by the gate and fall, and ran out and brought her in. She was shivering convulsively.

"He is gone," she gasped. "I saw him, but he is gone now! You must go! Why doesn't he come for you? Oh, what does it mean?"

He made her sit by the fire and drink some milk and talked soothingly, as to a frightened child.

"Poor girl! Three nights alone! No wonder you're imagining things!"

"I saw him! I saw him!" she repeated, trembling. "He was calling you! You must go."

"Calling me? I didn't hear a sound."

"No, but he had his hands to his mouth, and then he beckoned, frantically!"

"If it had been Andy he would have come in."

"I know, I know . . . Perhaps it wasn't . . . But it was somebody . . . I couldn't see . . . only you must go, now. Oh, for God's sake, go!"

Her voice was wild and broken, her eyes staring; she was shaking from head to foot; it was dreadful to see her like that. He spoke firmly: "I can't leave you like this."

Mary understood. She knew that so long as she seemed unnerved and shaken he would not go and she knew that he must go or die. And she knew, looking up at the kind, troubled face bent over hers, that his life was more precious than all the world.

She hid her face in her hands and strove to quiet her breathing—to keep the terror out of her voice. Then she looked up and said more steadily, "Won't you go, now?"

He straightened himself, relieved, but looked round, smiling:

"But where will I go to? 'Tis not very safe outside. And it's so good here by the fire. Surely you would not drive me out in the cold?"

His light tone sent terror to her heart again. "Oh, Mother of God, help me!" she moaned. "What will I do?"

"Whisht! Whisht!" his voice quieted her suddenly. His hand was on her shoulder. He stood erect. A low, tremulous call, wild and mournful, was rising from the bogs below. Mary knew it well; all her life she had heard it, wandering between the shore and the mountains—the curlew's cry.

Three times it was repeated and then three times again. Niell started to the door.

"It is Andy!" he exclaimed. "That's our signal! He's in trouble, wanting help—I must go!"

"The curlews do be crying when the tide ebbs," Mary said, "crying like souls in pain . . . But go, and God be with you!" she added quickly. "Stoop down! Don't show yourself! Hide in the quarries below!"

He gave one glance at her face and saw that the fear was gone from it.

"I'll be back," he said, and then he was gone.

&

Not a quarter of an hour had passed—Mary was still on her knees, praying, when the shouting and thundering came at the door.

"Open this door or we'll break it in!"

Mary drew the bolt, the soldiers rushed in with fixed bayonets. The officer had a revolver in his hand. With practiced celerity they dispersed themselves through the four rooms, and the opening of chests and cupboards, wrenching of boards and ripping of mattresses began.

"Who's in this house?" "Are there any men here?" "Where's the man that was here tonight?" The questions were flung at her. Mary replied to all quietly, "There's no one but myself."

She stood in the centre of the room, scarcely heeding them, untroubled and unafraid, wrapt in a dream. To the officer's bullying tones, the revolver pushed in her face, the jibes of the soldiers, she made brief, absent-minded replies. The officer lifted his hand, exasperated at last, and stuck her on the side of the head, and she raised grey eyes so childlike and wondering, filling with tears of pain, that he cursed himself and turned away.

The men were quieter after that and they left soon, without saying "goodnight".

She left the door ajar and crept into bed, and lay crying for a long time, tired out. But presently a strange sense of rest stole over her, of everything being well. It filled her body and her heart and soul—a drowsy knowledge of sweetness and wonder and safety greater than her life had known. Her whole being breathed that lovely fragrance and became one with it, and as dawn glimmered faintly behind her window, she slept.

જી

When, in full daylight, she put on a new blue dress and went into the sun-flooded kitchen, Niell was there. He had washed the dishes and set the table and had the pot boiling on the fire. All traces of the raid were cleared away.

"Thank God they didn't harm you!" he exclaimed when she came in. His face was very grave and pale.

"They were not too bad at all," she answered, longing to question him, yet feeling something withheld.

"What will you do now?" was all she asked.

"I will ask you," he said gently, "to go for me to Carrigrone and find Andy's brother. He—he will help to get me away."

He broke off and turned from her and stood looking into the fire. She could see how his hand clenched. It came to her that a great grief filled him and he thought to be keeping it from her.

"It is Andy," she said softly: "he is dead."

He held out his hand and she took it between her own, holding it strongly. His voice was low and strained.

"I found him—down by the quarries—shot through the head."

"I heard the shots that killed him," she said, slowly, "a little before you came."

"He was thinking about my safety only. He threw away his life for mine."

"And he kept you safe!" A light of great wonder lit Mary's face. "It is maybe the death that he would choose."

"He was the bravest boy . . ."

Niell sank down, struggling with flooding sorrow, but a calm shining wisdom was in Mary's eyes, as she looked over his bowed head to the sun.

The Black Banks

Mrs. O'Byrne stood at her door and watched the postman crossing the ford. The sun came out from behind a cloud and the glen was lit up suddenly with its wild yellow fires of gorse. Sweet and strong, the fragrance of it, in the warm sun. A soft wind was flowing down from the gap; the river was shallow after three days without rain and the stones under the water shone out like gold. It was when summer came all of a sudden, this way, that you would have pity for men working in dark mines.

A heaviness that had hung over her heart all the autumn and winter and wet spring, melted and fell away. If Jim had not written for seven weeks mightn't it well be that he'd struck gold at last and was coming home? Coming home with his money made, to marry and settle down and rear bonny children in the glen. In spite of the New World and its wonder that, she knew well, was ever and always a boy's dream.

" 'Tis for himself the letter is this week," Tom said. It had the American stamps and the black stripes across it, but the writing was not Jim's. There was a newspaper too. As she took them the heaviness fell again on her heart. She took them without a word and went in.

Mike was sitting in the corner smoking and resting himself. He was hardly able now for a day's work. The bridge he had started to build across the stream would never be finished, she was thinking, until Jim came home.

He took the letter and, putting on his spectacles, studied the address. Knowing his slow ways his wife, while she waited, set to work, shifting the kettle on the crane and pushing handfuls of bracken under it to bring it to the boil. She watched the dry brown fern smoke and kindle and blaze into windy flame and perish, each frond quivering red-gold for a moment before it crumbled to ash. Mike did not speak, the silence seemed to be swelling, the heaviness to be filling the room.

He held the letter out with a trembling hand, then sat with his head bowed and his hands clenched on the chair arms, quiet as a stone.

There had been an explosion. Jim was dead.

The wild cries and words that broke from her got no answer, no echo from her man. Bitterness against him rose up in her throat. She raised herself up and stood over him and let the long pain of the years find speech at last.

"Your foolishness and your greed that took him from me!" she broke out in deep, sobbing tones; "your pride that sent him to his death! What for did he want gold that had God's sunlight? Here now is the great future you said he'd gather? What good to him now is all your grand planning and he in a stranger's grave?"

The old man's head bent lower under the lash of her anger but he had no thought to be wounding her with his words. It was to himself he was moaning in his pain. "Mary to be lost to us and Jim buried. Not a son nor a daughter to come home to us in our old age, not a child nor a grandchild to leave after us to the world!"

She sank down on her knees and covered up her face with her hands and rocked to and fro in anguish; grief and remorse and fear were breaking over her, like the strong merciless waves of a dark sea.

"God's judgement on me it is," she cried, "for putting Mary away from me, for leaving a black curse on my own child . . . O Mary aroon, what will I do to get forgiveness? Mary, Mother of God, what will I do?"

Her desperate words made the old man lift his head. He had never heard words like that from her before. Ten long years it was now since Mary refused the good marriage they planned for her and went away for the Black Banks with her lover, taking with her her mother's curse. He himself loved his girl without changing, and prayed and waited, wanting only the chance to forgive her, but no word or token came. Never once was the girl's name mentioned between himself and his wife. They lived together with no other soul for company and that silence stretching between them like the black waste of the bog. He thanked God, in the midst of his sorrow, that the silence was broken now.

Kate had sunk down on the floor and was crying drearily, her head drooped in her arms on the chair. He got up laboriously and rested a hand on her shoulder, then moved away quietly to their room. The time he had been waiting for was come.

Under a loose board which he lifted easily a flat parcel lay, covered with dust. He brushed it and went back with it in his hands and sat down on the settle near his wife. "Kate," he said, "look what I have for you here. 'Tis a present I had waiting for you till the day you would forgive the girl. Will I be giving it to you now?"

At the wistful kindness in his voice her sobbing quieted; she looked up and nodded her head.

"Mr. Andrews made it for me," her husband said, pulling off the paper and string; "the painter, do you mind, that was stopping at Cole's. From an old photograph he did it, coloured and all. 'Tis a wonderful likeness. There it is for you now."

He stood up and set it on the chimney-piece, and the face smiled down at them gravely, a girl's face with soft brown eyes under long lashes, a wide forehead and dark brows and hair.

Tears streamed down the mother's face as she looked at it. She sat in the settle, gazing, putting a hand in her man's.

"Mary is dead too, Mike," she said. "I felt the knowledge of it these long years in my heart. 'If ever you bear a child may it destroy ye,' I said to her, 'the way you have destroyed me.' God forgive me, those were awful words. I think she died of them in a year."

Mike was silent. Kate gasped and trembled under the storm of her own remorse.

"What will I do," she cried out, "to get God's forgiveness? It is too late surely to make amends. What can you do for them you have driven from you? What can you do for the dead?"

Her husband sat down on the settle beside her and held her to him with a compassionate arm.

"We are getting our punishment in this world, surely," he said, heavily, "and God will forgive us in the next. To be waiting here alone in our weakness no son or daughter to come to us . . . To be drawing to the end and no child of the O'Byrne's to be growing while we fail . . . To be waiting lonely for our death."

The sweet face in the picture smiled down at them, unchanged by their grieving, while the sun sank behind clouds and the day darkened, and for mere age and weariness, they ceased, at last, to weep.

❦

A good drying day, with the sun and the warm breeze: Mrs. Walsh set the tub in the yard. She had a pain in her head that throbbed whenever she moved, but no matter, the washing had to be done.

Black mud on Patsy's shirt again where he fell in the bog. He did it to spite her, running up the mountain whenever she sent him to get turf. Some kind of demon had come into the boy since his father died and he had no hand over him but her own. With his father he used to be obedient enough. He could be good when he liked but he seemed to have set his mind now on crossing her. It was coming to a fight between them.

Screams and shrill voices came to her from the road: Aggie and Jack quarrelling: would Patsy quiet them now? A boy of his age should have that much sense. The time would come when she'd lose patience . . .

She wiped the suds from her arms and went out to the front. Aggie was red in the face with yelling and Jack had his head plastered with mud. Patsy was below with the buckets bringing up water from the well. He should have got that done an hour since.

"Why couldn't you mind the childer?" she asked him as he came up.

The boy's black brows drew together and he looked up at her with obstinacy written in every line of his white face.

"I was getting the water," he said; "I couldn't be doing two things at wonst."

The answer angered her.

"How many things do I have to be doing at wonst," she said sharply—"watching the pot and minding the childer and feeding the chickens and washing the clothes—striving to get the filth out of your clothes, you dirty little pig. 'Tis a pig-stye you ought to be living in and not a decent house."

Patsy said nothing, he turned with his buckets to the house. She called him back.

"Take them shoes off you till Sunday," she said. "I'll not slave day and night to keep you in shoe leather till I get some thanks for it. Playing yourself, I know you, down at the well."

108

Patsy set the buckets down on the road. His face was puckered and quivering. If he'd cry or say he was sorry, you could forgive him, but, instead, he put on his airs of defiance, squaring up to her.

"I was not playing myself," he said.

"You're a liar," was her answer to that. "I want none of your back-answering, bad or good. Take them children inside and clean them and then go up for the turf. And mind you're not late for your tea. If I have to give you another belting, 'twill be one you'll remember," she said, letting him off with a threat.

God knows it is hard, she was thinking, as she went on with her work, scrubbing the soiled shirt on the board—it is hard dealing with a head-strong, spiteful boy without the aid of a man. How to teach Patsy obedience she couldn't tell; you couldn't be forever beating a child; if she sent him without his tea to bed it made him walk in his sleep—he'd get out of the window again like last time and frighten the children out of their wits. As for talking to him, you might as well be battering your tongue on stone.

When the clothes were rinsed she sat down on a box in the yard and rested her aching head on her hands. The hardness of her life, the thought of long toilsome years in front of her, made her almost wish for death. What pleasure did she ever get out of life since the day she was born? Frank Walsh didn't marry her for love, he made no secret about that. He never ceased fretting for his dead wife. He took her because he wanted a woman to mind Patsy and they were not two years married before he died of pneumonia, leaving the boy on her hands.

"Keep Patsy, do your best for him . . . Don't send him way . . . His mother's people wouldn't be kind . . . " Those were his last words. She had given her promise, and kept it, and would keep it, with the help of god, however hard it might be.

If it was a bright handy boy who would be quick about the place and willing she wouldn't complain, and that would be grateful to her and do what he could. But a queer ailing little creature like that, with his secret, unnatural ways and his dark eyes. Her own children's eyes, thank God, were as blue as the sky.

Well no one would have it to say, all the same, that she wronged or neglected her husband's child.

She rose and took the clothes and hung them on the line; then she went in to get the children's tea.

ॐ

Patsy washed the children's faces and then, to make them quiet and good, pulled from under his mattress his one treasure, the only thing in the world that belonged to himself by right, a book of tales of the Heroes that his father had given him for a prize when he learned to read. The stories in it were too hard for Jack and Aggie, but they loved the coloured pictures of swans and magicians and horses and cats and battles and Patsy made up new stories about them—easy stories that they could understand. He grew happy himself, telling them. He was always happy when he was looking at the book—happy and—almost—good.

But he was wasting time and he had to go up to the Black Banks for turf. He stowed the book away in its secret place again and took the creel and went trailing it up the sunlit hill.

But he did not take off his shoes. He did not take off his shoes because Mrs. Walsh had told him to and because she had threatened him with a belting and called him a liar and a pig. She wanted to make him afraid of her, that was it. He remembered two things his Daddy taught him; one was to be obedient but the other was not to be afraid, and that was the most important, he thought. Lying was a part of being afraid. That's why he wouldn't lie to Mrs. Walsh, though he knew well she'd be glad if he would lie to her sometimes, instead of answering her right out. And she'd say he lied whether he did or not. He hated her, and he wouldn't take off his shoes.

The bog was all mossy and wet and warm. He could have loved to feel the wet ooze squelching through his toes. But he wouldn't take off his shoes. There were tiny yellow flowers opening among the roots of the grasses and the air was full of scents. The canawaun was shining in the sunlight, its silver hair all blowing one way. It looked, he thought, as if little wisps of morning mists had got caught in the grasses and were frightened and trying to fly away.

His father never brought him that way without telling him stories, and that was the way they loved best to come. When he was tired his father would carry him . . . He pretended to be tired sometimes, because it was so nice to be carried in those strong arms.

It was no good being tired now . . .

A big bursting pain came in his heart; he began crying to himself as he stumbled up the hill, dragging the creel. Crying was no good; nothing would ever be any good, but he cried. He was crying all the time while he worked at the Black Banks, filling the creel with sods.

୯ଠ

The black bog stretches along the whole ridge of the mountains between Killaderry and Glenbwee, except where the high stony summits rise, so that a traveller from the glen to the village, sooner than cross the mountains, would take a day's journey by the roads. But there are no travellers between them: for all the glen and the village knew of each other they might be a hundred leagues apart.

Some blight or curse, you would imagine, had blackened these mountain tops. Black, cracked and blistered, the turf in some spots, wet and slimy in others; trickles of thick black water creep through the crevices, rising out of bottomless pits of ooze. Here and there banks or hummocks of firm peat rise out of it, topped with grass, and to these, sometimes, sheep venture, though many a one has been drowned in the sucking bog.

Patsy's father had told him about it and warned him not to go there alone, and one day he took a stone and flung it into the bog and with his own eyes Patsy had seen it swallowed up. Then, lifting Patsy after him, he had gone, striding and leaping like a giant from hummock to hummock, and, making a zig-zag track on the bare stretches, climbed up to the ridge of the mountain and showed him the golden glen.

That Patsy remembered as the most wonderful thing that had ever happened to him and the glen as the grandest sight he had ever seen.

Out of a little blue loch that shone like a looking-glass, a white stream went racing down. Out of the mountain-side facing them a torrent of water fell, flinging its foam about as if a thousand snow-white ponies were shaking their manes . . . as if their manes were strung with a million silver bells. The mountain-sides were red with heather and the river edges blazing with yellow gorse; it was like drinking honey to breathe the sweet air . . . A great bird, the largest he had ever seen, went flying along the river into the glen: it was like a bird that carried Fidelma away from the cruel wizard into Tír-na-n-Óg . . . Everything was happy there; everyone in the glen was kind. His father never told him that, but Patsy knew. And he knew a glorious secret that his father did tell him—that the golden glen was his own.

"It is your Mother's country," Daddy had said; "it is the country of your Mother's people since God made Ireland." "Then it is my country," Patsy said, and his father had answered, "It is."

Not knowing the safe way over the black bog he would have to travel by the road. That would mean waiting till he grew strong and tall. The day he grew tall enough, he had decided, to reach the lowest rafter with his hand, he would put bread and meat in his pocket and set out. He would go to his country and his own people and never leave it any more.

When he had filled the creel with the heaviest load he could manage Patsy stood erect and looked around him, wiping the tears from his eyes with his sleeve.

The sun was high still, shining and warm. Shining blue the little lake would be, blazing gold the gorse. A bird flew up out of a hollow and sailed away over the ridge of the hill. A wild thought sprang up in Patsy's mind and his heard gave a leap. Over the banks, jumping the hummocks, tiptoe over the wide black stretches, the way his father went, he would go. He would look down at the lake and the glen.

What Mrs. Walsh would do to him he didn't care.

Nothing mattered except to see it—the strong foaming torrent and the gold—the country that was his own.

From tuft to tuft he jumped easily, giving whoops of joy. Soon he seemed to be near the top. But the grassy knolls were farther apart here and he had to run from one to another, lightly, quickly, expecting every minute to feel the surface give way. His own skill and daring the sense of the danger he was running and the price he would have to pay, and the exultant thought of the splendours he would be seeing, blew all the sorrow and pain out of his mind. He tingled from head to foot with joy.

The last hummock, the one they had stood upon where they looked down into Tír-na-n-Óg, lay far off, all alone, a green island in a black evil region of sucking bog. Carefully Patsy lowered himself from his grassy resting-place and stepped out, his brown eyes dark as the bogland with wonder and fear. He took two steps cautiously, safely, and started to run, but his leg went down suddenly, over the knee into peat and his other foot, when he swung his weight on to it, went in ankle deep. With a sob of terror he flung himself back, clutching at the grass he had left. He was just able to reach it and cling to it with his hands. There, stretched out, groping helplessly with his left foot for a foothold, he lay, while the mud sucked and sucked at his right leg. There was a slimy monster in it that wanted to swallow him up. He could feel it licking; it was pulling his shoe off. He worked his toes, trying to save it, but couldn't. In a minute he felt the shoe drawn off. His leg was sinking farther in.

His heart beat so hard that it choked him; a dark mist was coming before his eyes; he would have screamed, though there was no one to hear him, but he couldn't make his voice come. For hours it seemed to him he tugged and struggled there until at last, with a desperate straining heave he got himself up to the hummock and, running and leaping as though a demon were after him, came down again to his creel of turf.

❧

The supper was still on the table and Mrs. Walsh was out in the yard when Patsy stole in. He seized a bit of cold bacon and ate it and took a drink of milk. He had a good bit taken before she heard him and came in.

She had guessed, when he did not come home at teatime, that he was practising some deliberate act of disobedience

114

and she had made up her mind that the devil in him must be broken once and for all.

They stood facing one another, she dishevelled and exhausted from the day's toil, he wearing one shoe only black with peat water from head to foot, his eyes glowering sombrely in his white face.

He had been shaken and unnerved by his danger and he cowered before the queer wavering smile she had on her face.

"You have been in the bog," she said, with closed teeth.

He nodded, his throat was strangled.

"You have lost your new shoe."

He nodded again. His teeth had begun to chatter; he was cold.

"You thought you'd get the better of me, well we'll see. Strip off those clothes and wash yourself and get into bed."

He went out into the yard and stripped his muddy clothes off, leaving them in a bundle on the box. He washed himself well in the bucket that was in the yard. Then, putting on an old shirt, he got into bed and lay there shivering with cold.

He knew a thrashing was coming but it didn't frighten him much. To lie there shaking and not be able to quiet himself was what troubled him most of all. There was a glimmer of daylight still. He put his hand under the mattress and pulled out his book. Even to hold it, to lie with it under his cheek on the pillow, made him feel better, made him remember that he did possess one thing in the world that no other soul had a right to, and that he had a mother that loved him, and a father, though both were in Heaven, and that he had a golden glen of his own.

The shivering stopped and he leant up on one elbow and began to read the story of the fight at the ford. Even when the light was quite gone he went on, for he knew that story by heart. When he heard Mrs. Walsh come in and saw the light of the candle he stiffened, but he did not stir or look up.

With a sudden movement she stripped the blankets off his bed and he sprang up, kneeling, to defend himself. She had a thick leather strap in her hand. She saw the book lying on the pillow and her lifted arm fell to her side. The anger that had been hot in her turned to anger that was stone cold.

"So that is all your care," she said. "You come in with your heart as black as your clothes with sinful disobedience and instead of crying for your wickedness you lie reading stories in your bed. 'Tis that cursed book," she cried shrilly, "that puts the bad thoughts in your mind," and catching it up, she ran with it to the kitchen. Patsy heard her stirring the fire to a blaze.

Horror held him frozen for a moment, then he flung himself from his bed and rushed out. He flew at her, hitting, kicking, biting, catching her by the hair, but she dropped the book in the flames and got him down. She held him down with her knee on his back and he saw it burn, saw the leaves curl up and fly up the chimney in grey flakes, flaming, and all that was left fell into grey ash.

He screamed and writhed convulsively till it had perished, then the strength went out of him and he lay still.

Mrs. Walsh stood up then; her head was sore, her face bruised; her wrist was bleeding from the boy's savage teeth.

"Tomorrow," she said, looking down at him, "I'll give you your payment for this. I haven't the strength tonight."

Then she turned the lamp out and went to bed.

The last glow died out of the fire as Patsy lay there. The shawl he had pulled off Mrs. Walsh in the combat was beside him on the floor, he wrapped it around himself and lay still. He wanted never to get up again. "Couldn't you make me die and come to you," he whispered, as he lay there. "Oh Mother Mary, couldn't you make me die?"

It was his own fault, they were saying to him, for losing his new shoe. It was because he did that that Mrs. Walsh had destroyed them all. Maybe if he found it they would all come alive again. He should go for it, Cúchulainn said. But he *was* looking for it, everywhere, everywhere, and he couldn't find it at all. All night he was looking for it in the dark. It was deep, deep down under the bog. He was dipping his hands into the bog and he couldn't find it. He was swimming about looking for it under the black mud. He couldn't find it, and he was sleepy . . . He couldn't open his eyes . . .

He tried harder and opened his eyes at last and saw bright stars over his head and felt a cool wind around his bare legs. He had the shawl clutched tightly about him over his shirt. He couldn't see where he was. He must have walked out in his sleep . . .

Under his feet there was short wet grass. He stood quite still, there was not a sound anywhere—not the least, faintest shadow of a sound . . . A cloud was drawing away from the moon.

The cloud passed; the moon was a thick crescent like a cow's horn. A pale ghostly light lay on the world. A nightmare terror seized him and he crouched down. He was on a lonely little island of grass; all around him and far and wide stretched the black horrible bog. He was in the place where he had lost his show. He could see, in the moonlight, the huge greedy monster, heaving under the bog; it was winding itself like a serpent around the hummock of turf. It was waiting to swallow him. Perhaps it couldn't come up on to the grass. He pulled the dark shawl right over him and curled himself up as small as he could, breathing so quietly that it couldn't hear. He felt sure it couldn't come up on to the green grass.

It was dark and warm under the shawl—dark and warm and safe. Perhaps he would go to sleep there . . . He was so sleepy . . . He wouldn't be afraid . . . Mother Mary would keep him safe . . .

She was talking to him softly, in a little whispering voice like the stream. She was lifting him in her arms and wrapping her dark shawl round him and telling him to come with her. He was running along the air, holding her hand.

She talked to him in her gentle, loving voice, like running water; sometimes she seemed to be carrying him in her arms and he was little and light. She told him all his stories over again, the swan-maiden flew by them, Fionualla, flying over Tír-na-n-Óg, and she lifted them up on her sleek, silvery wings. She flew with them along the river, into the glen. Then he was walking on cold dewy moss again, with a thousand stars overhead, with Mother Mary's shawl wrapped round him and his hand holding her hand.

Her face was the sweetest face he had ever seen, pale in the moonlight, smiling, looking down at him with the dark, beautiful eyes, full of kindness and love. He did not have to look where he was going or even to keep awake; he hid his face in her shawl again and let dreams come.

☙

A hot light shining on his eyelids made Patsy open his eyes at last. He was full of tiredness and happiness—such tiredness and happiness as he had never felt in all his life before.

The first thing he saw was a great gorse bush growing by his head; thick and heavy with yellow blossoms it was; he watched a bee burrowing into the deep, sweethearted flowers.

It was among soft bracken that he was lying and tall ferns were all round him; he could hear the river close at his ear, laughing and making the sound of bells. He stood up, all weak and shaky and looked around him at the sunlit glen.

He saw the mountains with the white thin mists blowing over them slowly, and the boulders and the red fields of heather and torrents tumbling down into the river, and the river with its edges of blazing gorse.

A little row of trees stood near him and behind the trees were the white walls of a house.

He stood watching the house, too weak to move, until smoke began to waver up from the chimney into the blue air. He knew then that he was hungry, more hungry than he had ever been before, so hungry that he could scarcely walk.

There was a smooth field between him and the trees. He crossed it and crossed the road and went into the yard and sat down on the steps of the house, leaning his head against the wall. He could hear someone moving about inside and he knocked with his fists on the door. Footsteps shuffled toward him; the latch was lifted and the door opened and an old woman looked out. She didn't see him at first and he laughed; he laughed up at her sitting on the steps, and she looked down and cried out and went down on her knees beside him and looked into his face with her eyes all wide and frightened and then caught him and hugged him in her arms.

He felt so weak he couldn't answer the questions they were asking him, herself and the old man. He sat in a big chair by the fire while they talked to one another and fed him with bread and milk. They seemed to be crying and happy at the same time. It was a wide cosy room they were in, with coloured delph on the dresser and a big clock.

"How did you find your way to us, *acushla*?" they were asking. "Was it a miracle brought you to us, son?"

He was gazing, his pale face alight, at the picture over the chimney-piece.

"There she is," he whispered. "Mother Mary, she came to me. She brought me over the bog . . ."

The old woman took him on her knee then and sat with him by the fire, crooning over him, and praying and giving thanks to God and His Holy Mother, until with the warmth and the tiredness and the wonder that were over him Patsy fell asleep again.

The Venetian Mirror

"Is it the handwriting of a maniac?"

"A maniac? On the contrary!" I exclaimed at the first glance. The letter which Desmond had offered me for "diagnosis", as he called my graphology, was dated more than twelve months back from Milan. It was written on thin paper with a fine-pointed pen. It was a request, expressed in stately English, with a curious mixture of dignity and appeal, that the writer might be permitted to visit my friend in his Alpine solitude "with a view to persuading you to allow me to purchase an article sold to you by the trustees of my property in Ravenna four years ago—an article the possession of which is vital to my peace—even to my sanity—of mind." It was signed with the name of a great Italian family, by whose wish, however, the name is not to be disclosed.

The style of the letter was intriguing, the calligraphy even more so.

"On the contrary," I replied to Desmond's question, "it is the writing of a logician, severely intellectual and analytic. There is, however, a controlled nervousness in the script—I use 'nervousness', of course, in the medical sense—"

"Go on," Desmond urged, sitting forward in his chair. "I want to hear all you can make out. Then I have something to tell you."

"An extraordinarily interesting character," was my conclusion. "The self-command and artistic sensitiveness of

121

a highly-cultured personality seem to be balanced against something passionate, almost primitive . . . Should the balance be over-set," I added, "it is conceivable that mental derangement might result."

"Mental derangement?" Desmond repeated meditatively. "Yes . . . " Then he looked up at me with his odd, dry little smile. "Did you ever suspect me of incipient lunacy, Jim?"

"I have suspected you of many things, Avic," I answered, "but not, so far, of that."

"If the Count was mad, I was mad," he said then.

He was looking up at the loveliest of the many beautiful things which he had accumulated to cheer his exile in the snows—a mirror framed in gesso work, an enchantingly moulded garland of fruit and flowers. The glass was slightly convex, its form a perfect round. The rich paint and gilding of the frame were dimmed with age, but nothing could exceed the grace and tenderness of the design: the artist had fashioned it, you might imagine, to frame one loved face.

It hung alone at the end of the room on a canvas-covered wall. A long altar-table below it held candles in an antique sconce which, lighted now, made the mirror bloom out in the twilight like a great, luminous rose.

"It was your mirror that he wanted?" I said.

"Yes, it was the mirror . . . the poor old man!"

"And you refused to sell it?"

"No, no! How could I, in the circumstances, refuse?"

"Are you going to tell me the story or are you not?"

Desmond laughed. "Yes, I am going to tell you—since you swear you never thought me mad."

Desmond was better than when I last visited him—no doubt about that. That precious young life, which I had despaired of three years ago, was going to be saved.

It was with a sense of great contentment that I settled down in a deep chair by the wood fire to hear his tale.

"I bought the mirror five or six years ago," he said, "in a solitary old house in the forest between Venice and Ravenna—'Ravenna's immemorial wood . . .'

"The house was falling into decay; so were the old couple who took care of it. The trustees were selling the furniture and converting the house into a saw-mill, I believe. No one would live in it; there was some melancholy legend . . . I could learn no details at the time.

"It all struck me as rather tragic. The rooms remained just as their owner had left them, and nothing more exquisite could be conceived. The bedroom in which this mirror hung might have been the bridal-chamber of a queen.

"I paid more than I could afford for the mirror—I would have beggared myself sooner than let it go; and during that winter when I was so ill, when you banished me here and I nearly perished of home-sickness, it was my mirror of Shalott.

"I used to lie on the couch there, watching it, all that endless spring. It reflected the snow-mists that rose from the mountain, and the sky. I used to be pretending to myself that the Shatzalp was Carrantuohill . . . Watching the clouds drift past and change and shape themselves was the only occupation I had energy for then. I liked seeing the vermilion flush come on them at sunset and fade to violet and dull blue, until the twilight made all one, and my mirror hung in the dusk like a full moon.

"It was then, in the dead quiet and loneliness, before Giuseppe came in to light the candles, when the mirror gathered a soft, wan radiance into itself, that I used to see her face.

"It was her hair, I suppose, that made the faint, cloudy aura: it seemed to fly out wide, light as vapour, floating around her head, pale and gold. I never saw her face for more than a moment, and those moments were ecstasies of wonder and pain: her face was so young and piteous, and her beauty was beyond anything words could tell."

He paused. I was watching him closely, astonished, but he seemed lost in his memories and did not look up.

"Nearly every night she came for a while," he continued, "but her eyes never met mine. She seemed to be looking past or through me in unappeasable longing, for someone who was not there.

" 'Rest in peace, sweet soul!' I used to say . . . But all day I would wait hungrily for her coming, holding Death at arm's length, sometimes, only to see her again.

"When I grew stronger she ceased to come.

"I missed her inexpressibly—not as one misses a place or a person, rather as you miss the creatures of your own imagination after you have finished a book. I began to think of her, at last, as a creation of my own. Then, out of the void, that letter came."

"You knew nothing at all, previously," I interrupted, "about this man whose treasures you had bought?"

"Nothing. At the time of the sale he was regarded as non-existent. I thought him dead. That was explained later on.

"Have you ever felt the shock of an earth tremor? The coming of the letter was like that. The thought of losing the mirror threw me, literally, into a fever. I had the contempt-ible idea at first of not replying to it at all. Then I thought of simply refusing an interview—saying that I received no visitors here and would not sell. But the wording of his re-quest made it seem brutal to do that. I sat on that couch, in the dark, for hours, in a state of agitation that I suppose was childish. I had a conviction that if the Italian once crossed my threshold he would have his way with me.

" 'The mirror is mine: I bought it,' I said to myself, and felt a very Shylock in saying the words. It was not mine: I had no right to it; I knew that in my heart and soul.

"You know how you can gaze into a glass until oblivion drowns you. I think I was looking into it like that, seeking the heart of its mystery . . . I remember something like a breath appearing in it—a faint, luminous cloud; I saw that it was the light, honey-golden cloud of her hair. Then I saw her face as before, so pale, so forlorn and afraid . . . Her eyes, soft as a child's, were wide with trouble; her lips were parted a little; her breath seemed held . . .

"As though my sight were failing me, the image faded.

"I lit candles and answered the letter then, begging the Count to do me the honour of visiting me for a few days.

"I wish I had not lost the letter in which he replied. His thanks were charmingly expressed. 'I come as one hermit to another,' he wrote. I felt eager, in spite of my apprehension, to meet the old man.

"It was on an April evening, in the thick of a sudden snow-storm that I heard the bells of his sleigh coming up.

"The man servant who accompanied him, and who helped him out of his furs, was terribly concerned at his having been exposed to the snow.

"The Count took my hand and thanked me for receiving him in a manner at once courtly and impulsive. His whole personality struck me instantly as having something in it—some pleasant quality—a quarter of a century out of date.

"It would have been difficult to tell his age. He stooped a good deal, but from illness or scholarly habits, one would guess. His face was very thin, delicate and austere, with deep eye-sockets and high cheek-bones. His lips, closely pressed together, were full of sensitive life—of suffering, was my first thought.

"He had the most beautiful hands I have ever seen.

"In spite of his look of inbred and inherited authority there was something hesitant, dependent, in his way of looking about him; one felt that he needed care.

"I conducted him at once to his own room.

"My intention was to leave the question of the mirror untouched until the morning and not to open this room till then.

"We dined in the breakfast room.

"At dinner, I remember, he talked about Ireland, and astonished me by his comprehension. He passed to reminiscences of the Risorgimento and of Mazzini.

" 'It is a Mazzini, is it not,' he said 'that Ireland needs?'

"I agreed.

" 'But you will not agree with me,' he said then, smiling, 'when I suggest that it is your incorrigible belief in a future existence that makes you too apt to failure in this?'

" 'You have no faith, then,' I asked him frankly, 'in an existence after death?'

"He smiled as he answered: 'I have had no evidence of it,' but a sudden spasm of anguish fixed the smile, so that his face, for a moment, was like a tragic mask.

"He looked fragile and tired in the extreme, but when, after dinner, I suggested that he might wish to retire, disappointment brought a flush to his cheeks. I realised that I must bring him to the mirror at once.

"When I had lit the candles I brought him into this room. He was exerting intense self-control. The stick on which he leaned with both hands shook under him, and his breath came between clenched teeth.

" 'It is very lovely, is it not?' he said to me in measured tones; then he collapsed into that chair, trembling, and sank his face down between his hands.

"I knew then, past all doubt or remedy, that the mirror was no longer mine.

" 'It is so lovely,' I answered, 'and its beauty means so much to me, that no offer of money could make me part with it.'

"He lifted a face so pallid, eyes so despairing, that I added instantly: 'But if you can convince me that you have a right to it beyond question of purchase, it is yours.'

"His face relaxed.

" 'I was prepared to ask you,' he said slowly, 'to name your own price.'

" 'It is too beautiful to be bartered,' I answered. 'I could not take for it one lira more than I paid.'

"He rested those melancholy eyes of his on mine, searchingly; then a very sweet and trustful smile lit up his face.

" 'It is my full confidence that I must give you, then,' he said, and I replied that his confidence was what I asked.

"He sat erect in his chair, his face calm and pale, while he told me that awful story—a story of passion and violence more fitting to the days of the Borgias or the Medici than to our own time.

"Thirty years before he had brought home to that forest villa of his a young Venetian bride. The girl's father had promised her to a wealthy and swaggering Roman whom she abhorred. The lovers were married secretly by some good Friar Lawrence, and fled from Venice at dawn. They believed that, the deed once done, the Count's name would be a protection, and that they would be unmolested in their forest home. They made the perilous journey through Chioggia and Ariano, and reached the Pineta on the third day.

"At nightfall they came to the villa which he had prepared for her like some palace in a fairy-tale. One treasure of her own, besides gowns and jewels, she had already smuggled from her father's house—the mirror which was an heirloom in her dead mother's family, and which had been her childhood's first delight. It was already hung in the bridal-chamber between the windows, lit up with tall candles, when she came in.

"The old man had half-forgotten me as he recalled how his bride sat before the mirror combing her spun-gold hair, singing some wild little song for joy of freedom and love, while he stood by her side, smiling at her reflection when their eyes met.

"He heard a sound below, and stepped out on to the balcony and looked down. Tall pine-trees shaded the lawn; the night was starless; he saw nothing, heard nothing, but the song of a nightingale in the undergrowth and the cicalas in the grass. He came to his bride again.

"He was standing behind her, drawing her lovely hair out between his fingers, when he heard the clangour of the gate-bell and knocking below.

"The tired servants were abed; he turned to go down himself.

" 'Don't stay long away from me; I shall be lonely in this strange place,' his bride pleaded. He smiled reassuringly to her troubled face in the mirror. Then he went down.

"It was a friar, or so he seemed, who came, with some inconsequent message from the bride's father; he was garrulous, and held the Count long in talk.

"As the young lover ran up the stairs again a terrible apprehension seized his heart. His call evoked no answer. When he opened the door the room was in darkness, empty; the table was overset, the windows open, the window-curtain torn down.

"The girl was found three days later, dead, at the bottom of a precipitous gorge, above which a horse-path ran. She had thrown herself down to escape from her abductor, it was believed.

"The Count pursued the young Roman like a bloodhound for a month, while the slow processes of the law crawled on. He found him hiding in a hut in a lonely part of the Adriatic coast. He dragged him out and flung him over a cliff.

" 'I was a strong man then,' he said.

"He went back to his forest home and lived in the basement, shutting out the light of day. Life had become a loathsome nightmare, yet he thought suicide unworthy of himself. He lived like a stricken animal, brooding there. The idea of her exquisite intelligence, her gay, sweet bravery, her tenderness, dashed out, like a quenched candle, on those stones—all that composed her loveliness buried in the earth, 'to lie in cold corruption and to rot . . .' Such thoughts to him who knew, as he said, that there is no soul . . .

"He had the mirror brought down and hung in his dusty room and burned candles before it in the dark. He was experimenting, cynically, in the workings of his own mind, in the 'faculty for self-hypnosis which has created all the religions in the world.'

" 'It is not strange, you will admit,' he said to me, 'that at last hallucinations came . . . Dreams—in sleep I would see her, singing, brushing her shining hair—waking, I would see her face looking out at me from the mirror, piteous, afraid, and pale.'

" 'Do not stay long from me,' she seemed always to be saying; 'I am lonely in this strange place.'

" 'Hallucinations!' the old man muttered. 'Ah, how sweet they were, yet how fearful! I knew the truth then—that I was mad. I gave myself up to my madness with a sort of perverse joy. I surrendered myself to the authorities, confessing my crime. I have been in mad-houses and in prisons for seven and twenty years.'

"You can guess, Jim, how I felt, hearing that," Desmond said.

"This old man, with a face like Dante, every motion of whose soul and body was under tense intellectual control, had given himself to be shut up in mad-houses and in prisons because he saw—what I myself had seen—had seen, remember, only the night before."

"And he wanted the mirror again!" I exclaimed. "Good God, Desmond—what did you do?"

"Nothing at first; I felt helpless; I sat staring into the fire, waiting for the chaos to settle itself in my brain.

"The Count went on talking. He had completely recovered his sanity within a short time, he said, and had spent the years in prison planning a philosophical work— an 'Atheistic Philosophy', educing a code of virtue from natural law, independent of the ideas of God, religion and a soul. I was his intention to devote his remaining years to the completion and publication of this work.

"I think he got the notion, from my silence that I was going to refuse. A note of pleading came into his talk. He told me how, when the prison gates were opened, he travelled home to find every treasure, every symbol of his past life scattered to the winds.

"Everything else he was satisfied to let go, but he set himself to trace the mirror as he had once set himself to track a man. By following clues that were mere rumours and reminiscences, for ten months, he had found me out.

" 'You think all this but a madman's whim!' he exclaimed, humbly, appealingly, at last. 'Think it so then! And think that only by possessing that mirror again, by living in its presence and finding within it no image but my own, can my recovery, my sanity, be assured! If it is a madman's whim, will not you, in pity, in charity, humour it?'

"I hated to hear the old man talk like that. I began pacing about the room. The excitement was devastating. To know that we had seen this thing, he and I—to know such things could be! It was like the opening of a window on to a light too strong for mortality to endure.

"Then my responsibility to my guest! To refuse the mirror seemed impossible; to give it to him might be to fling him into madness again—if he had ever been mad; into the delusion of it, if he had not. I could not bring myself to speak to him of what I had seen. I felt there would be an indelicacy, a presumption amounting to sacrilege, in doing that . . .

"At length, however, perhaps from sheer nervous exhaustion, the burden slid away from me. There were forces at work in this, I decided, undreamed of in our philosophy. I would leave the solution to them.

" 'The mirror is yours, Count,' I said; 'I surrender it to you. I beg for your friendship in return.'

"He laid his hand in mine to rise from his chair. His emotion was beyond his control; his lips quivered; his eyes filled with tears.

"I took down the mirror and hung it in the Count's room and placed the candles, lighted, on a table under it. His man, who was waiting for him anxiously, was dismissed to bed. The Count drew back the heavy curtains and looked out for a while at the empty, snow-muffled night.

"He turned to me at last.

" 'It will take me many years to thank you, my friend,' he said.

"Then I left him alone.

"I sat up in this room with the door open; I knew that something must happen . . . How could I guess what it would be?"

Desmond broke off; an expression of acute distress contracted his face.

"Would you say I did wrong, Jim, leaving him with it like that, nothing told?"

" 'It is easy for the fool to be wise,' I quoted, 'after the event.' It is hard to see what else you could do . . . As you say, there were higher powers . . . "

Then I asked: "He went mad, there, in that room?"

"No," Desmond answered. "No, thank God. I heard nothing. The house was as still as the dead world out-side.

131

I sat there until dawn, listening; then I went out and softly opened his door. The candles were guttering out under the mirror; the Count was lying before it, full length on the floor. He was dead. You would say, from the look on his face, he had died of joy."

The dark vitreous blue of the Alpine twilight had closed over us as we talked. The mirror in its lustrous frame hung glimmering, like a haloed moon.

"It is yours still, then?" was all I could find to say.

"Yes," Desmond answered; "but it is empty now."

"May they rest in peace," I said, and Desmond responded, "Amen!"

Acknowledgements

The publisher would like to thank the following people
for their help with the preparation of this book:
Douglas A. Anderson, Richard Dalby, Peter Berresford
Ellis, Emma Flynn, Brian Gallagher, Meggan Kehrli,
Ken Mackenzie, Terri Neil, Jim Rockhill,
Sam Tranum, and Scott Valeri.

Earth-Bound: Nine Stories of Ireland
was first published by The Harrigan Press
(Worcester, Massachusetts) in December 1924.

ℰᴐ

"Earth-Bound" was first published in
The Dublin Magazine, December 1923.

"Samhain" was first published in
The Dublin Magazine, October 1924.

"The Prisoner" was first published
with the title "The Prisoners (1798-1923)"
in *Éire: The Irish Nation*, 13 September 1924 .

"By God's Mercy" was first published in
*The Irish World and the American
Industrial Liberator*, October 1924.

"A Story Without an End" was first published in
The Dublin Magazine, July 1924.

"Mountjoy" was first published in
Éire: The Irish Nation, 2 June 1923.

"Captivity" and "On Leaving Mountjoy"
were first published in
Éire: The Irish Nation, 9 June 1923.

"Escape" was first published in
Sinn Féin (New Series), 20 December 1924

"The Curlew's Cry" was first published in
Columbia (USA), June 1925.

"The Black Banks" was first published in
Columbia (USA), January 1926.

"The Venetian Mirror" was first published in
The Dublin Magazine, November 1924.

About the Author

Dorothy Macardle (1889-1958)—historian, playwright, journalist, and novelist—was born in Dundalk, Co. Louth. She was educated at Alexandra College in Dublin where she later lectured in English literature. She is best remembered for her seminal treatise on Ireland's struggle for independence, *The Irish Republic* (1937), but also wrote novels of the uncanny, including *The Uninvited* (1941), *The Unforeseen* (1946), and *Dark Enchantment* (1953). She died in Drogheda and is buried in St. Fintan's Cemetery, Sutton.

SWAN RIVER PRESS

Founded in 2003, Swan River Press is an independent publishing company, based in Dublin, Ireland, dedicated to
gothic, supernatural, and fantastic literature. We specialise in limited edition hardbacks, publishing fiction from
around the world with an emphasis on Ireland's contribu-
tions to the genre.

www.swanriverpress.ie

*"Handsome, beautifully made volumes . . .
altogether irresistible."*

– Michael Dirda, *Washington Post*

*"It [is] often down to small, independent, specialist presses to
keep the candle of horror fiction flickering . . . "*

– Darryl Jones, *Irish Times*

*"Swan River Press has emerged as one of the most inspir-
ing new presses over the past decade. Not only are the books
beautifully presented and professionally produced, but they
aspire consistently to high literary quality and originality,
ranging from current writers of supernatural/weird fiction to
rare or forgotten works by departed authors."*

– Peter Bell, *Ghosts & Scholars*

THE GREEN BOOK
Writings on Irish Gothic,
Supernatural and Fantastic Literature

edited by
Brian J. Showers

Aimed at a general readership and published twice-yearly, *The Green Book* features commentaries, articles, and reviews on Irish Gothic, Supernatural and Fantastic literature.

Certainly favourites such as Bram Stoker and John Connolly will come to mind, but *The Green Book* also showcases Ireland's other notable fantasists: Fitz-James O'Brien, Charlotte Riddell, Lafcadio Hearn, Rosa Mulholland, J. Sheridan Le Fanu, Cheiro, Harry Clarke, Dorothy Macardle, Lord Dunsany, Elizabeth Bowen, C. S. Lewis, Mervyn Wall, Conor McPherson . . . and many others.

> "*A welcome addition to the realm of accessible
> nonfiction about supernatural horror.*"
>
> – Ellen Datlow

> "*Eminently readable . . . [an] engaging little journal
> that treads the path between accessibility and
> academic depth with real panache.*"
>
> – Peter Tenant, *Black Static*

BENDING TO EARTH
Strange Stories by Irish Women

edited by Maria Giakaniki
and Brian J. Showers

Irish women have long produced literature of the gothic, uncanny, and supernatural. *Bending to Earth* draws together twelve such tales. While none of the authors herein were considered primarily writers of fantastical fiction during their lifetimes, they each wandered at some point in their careers into more speculative realms—some only briefly, others for lengthier stays.

Names such as Charlotte Riddell and Rosa Mulholland will already be familiar to aficionados of the eerie, while Katharine Tynan and Clotilde Graves are sure to gain new admirers. From a ghost story in the Swiss Alps to a premonition of death in the West of Ireland to strange rites in a South Pacific jungle, *Bending to Earth* showcases a diverse range of imaginative writing which spans the better part of a century.

"Bending to Earth *is full of tales of women walled-up in rooms, of vengeful or unforgetting dead wives, of mistreated lovers, of cruel and murderous husbands.*"

– Darryl Jones, *Irish Times*

"*A surprising, extraordinary anthology featuring twelve uncanny and supernatural stories from the nineteenth century . . . highly recommended, extremely enjoyable.*"

– British Fantasy Society

NOT TO BE TAKEN
AT BED-TIME
and Other Strange Stories

Rosa Mulholland

In the late-nineteenth century Rosa Mulholland (1841-1921) achieved great popularity and acclaim for her many novels, written for both an adult audience and younger readers. Several of these novels chronicled the lives of the poor, often incorporating rural Irish settings and folklore. Earlier in her career, Mulholland became one of the select band of authors employed by Charles Dickens to write stories for his popular magazine *All the Year Round*, together with Wilkie Collins, Elizabeth Gaskell, Joseph Sheridan Le Fanu, and Amelia B. Edwards.

Mulholland's best supernatural and weird short stories have been gathered together in the present collection, edited and introduced by Richard Dalby, to celebrate this gifted late Victorian "Mistress of the Macabre".

"It's a mark of a good writer that they can be immersed in the literary culture of their time and yet manage to transcend it, and Mulholland does that with the tales collected here."

– David Longhorn, *Supernatural Tales*